WOUNDS
by
Barbara Bockman

Copyright © 2013 by Barbara Bockman. All rights reserved.

No part of this book shall be reproduced or transmitted in any form or means, electronic, mechanical, magnetic, photographic including photocopying, recording or by any information storage and retrieval system, without prior written permission of the author.

This is a work of fiction. Names, characters, places and incidents either are the product of the author's imagination or are used fictitiously. Any resemblance to actual events or locales or persons, living or dead, is entirely coincidental.

ISBN: 978-1-936634-22-4

WOUNDS

Chapter One

> *"Oh, Tree, oh, Tree, I see in you ten thousand trees."*
> Ch'iu-it Liu

Craig slammed the back door with a bang. He ducked under the clothesline and dashed into the woods. No way he was going to stick around for another broken rib. He didn't look back to see if his dad was following. His eye puffed up and he spit out salty blood, but he held back the tears. He couldn't take it anymore! He clenched his jaw. "I'm never going back."

Craig stumbled. Those blasted old work boots. He hated wearing hand-me-downs. More determined, he plunged on, following the ancient path through the woods. He leaned against a tree, turned and looked back, gasping for breath. His house was out of sight and there was no sign of his dad.

"He can't chase me," Craig muttered. "Stupid drunk."

In the other direction, Craig made out the house of his neighbors, the Arks. It was bigger than his house, a small rental on the Ark property. The Ark home was nice, with green lawns and neat flowerbeds. An attached garage blended in with the nineteenth-century design.

Woods surrounded the property on three sides, but a solitary and grand oak tree dominated the near corner of the back lawn.

That was some awesome tree. Mr. Ark claimed it was a sapling when Columbus voyaged to the New World. It had been in his family since before the Civil War. Craig and Mr. Ark's son, Nelson, had measured the oak. The sixty-five-foot tall tree cast a noontime shadow long enough to shade four school buses placed end-to-end. The trunk was twenty-seven feet around.

Craig's troubled mind slipped a gear, and he was once again a little kid playing pirate in the spars of the oak with his friend, Nelson Ark.

* * * *

"Make 'im walk the plank, Cap'n." Nelson wore one of his mother's old red bandanas and a black eye patch left over from some Halloween.

From high up in the tree, Craig brandished a plastic sword. "I will, Matey, but first I'll hang 'im from the yardarm!"

"Hit the deck, you pirates," called a man's voice from below. Mr. Ark approached the tree with rakes and plastic bags and a chain saw. "Now you're landlubbers."

"Aw, Dad," said Nelson. "We were just getting started. Can't the raking wait till some other time?"

"Sorry, son." Mr. Ark's tone was sympathetic, but firm. "You've already put it off a week. Now get it over with. Consider yourself lucky live oaks don't drop all their leaves at once."

"Come on, Matey," Craig said to Nelson. "I'll help, too." He lowered himself to the next branch. "We'll rake now and finish off those black'ards some other time."

With his lower lip sticking out in a pout, Nelson followed Craig down. From the last branch six feet up, they used the rope ladder to reach the ground. "Thanks, Craig," said Mr. Ark. "You boys bag the leaves and put the rakes back into the tool shed when you're done."

"Okay, Dad," Nelson said.

"And, Nelson," added Mr. Ark, "put your bike in the garage."

Craig tossed his plastic sword aside. "Bet I can fill more bags than you can," he challenged.

Nelson ripped the bandana and eye patch off and grabbed a rake. "Bet you can't!"

"I'm going into the forest to cut some firewood," Mr. Ark said. "I'll call you to help carry it when I get a stack."

In a few minutes, a distant metallic buzzing droned over the swish of the rakes in the dry leaves.

After a while, Nelson's mom came out to the back porch, followed by a low slung, reddish-brown dog and two cats. She carried a tray. "Cookies and lemonade, boys."

"Let's take a break, Craig." Nelson took the porch steps two at a time. "I'm thirsty."

"Thanks, Mrs. Ark." Craig wiped his hands on his shorts before he accepted a glass.

"Good cookies, Mom."

Mrs. Ark said, "Would you like to stay for supper,

Craig? I called your mother and she said you may."

"I sure would, Mrs. Ark." Craig smiled. "Thank you." It was always a treat for Craig to eat here. It wasn't that his mom wasn't a good cook. She just didn't have all the good stuff Mrs. Ark did.

"Woof," said the dog, looking up at Nelson.

"Not too many sweets for you, Siegfried." Nelson gave him a piece of cookie and scratched his neck. "We got to keep you lean and mean."

Craig picked up a chewed-on tennis ball and threw it into the yard. "Go, fetch, Siegfried."

"He'll go get the ball, but he won't give it back to you," Nelson said. "Dachshunds are real stubborn. When they get attached to something they grip it like a nut wrenched to a bolt."

"Nelson," said Mrs. Ark, "don't forget, you have a K'BeTs meeting after dinner." Craig didn't belong to K'BeTs—Kids for a Better Tomorrow—because his family didn't have money for extras, like clubs.

Going back into the house, Mrs. Ark was again followed by the two cats. Siegfried stayed out to play tag with the rakes then he stretched out in the autumn sun for a nap.

The boys raked and bagged until Mr. Ark came back and asked them to help him carry and stack the firewood. "This will feel real good next winter," he said.

"And smell good, too," said Craig, following him into the woods.

Through all the activity, the play, the work, and the

talk, Craig remembered the tree standing regal as a king, more massive than any tree around. There was grandeur and richness in this tree. It was special.

Mr. Ark bragged that strangers detoured from the highway for a glimpse of this tree—to marvel at its size and age. The Arks hosted a big picnic every summer for all the folks around. What fun boys and girls had climbing into its branches and playing house, or cowboy, or astronaut, or pirate as Craig and Nelson did. It was kind of a community tree.

* * * *

Now a rumbling noise penetrated Craig's dreamstate. The door of the garage swung upward. Mrs. Ark drove away, with Siegfried's nose sticking out the car window. Craig crashed back to reality. *Why did I let my mind wander? All of that good stuff was over a year ago. I don't want any warm, fuzzy feeling.* He let the anger come back, flowing like acid through the happy memories; he welcomed it. Anger was his ally; a part of him. It gave him strength and he wasn't going to let anything take it from him. What did he care if Nelson had a nice house? A kind dad? A mom?

What made Nelson so special that he had pets and a bike and a CD player? Video games and Wiis?

Craig clenched his fists, watching the car head for town. He touched his tender eye. It really hurt now; and his lip. Hot tears scalded the inside of his eyes and burned his nose, but he refused to release them. The ordeal of it all, the beatings, the broken dishes, the sour vomit he had to clean up after his dad, the embarrassment at school—a year of grief and torment was stored in Craig's heart. Pain flooded his veins, and he turned that pain into hatred. He would not let it out in tears, but he would let it out.

Craig swallowed the tears away. The heat now turned to cold and his heart became a lump of ice. The muscles of his face twisted into a sneer.

And what was so special about that old tree? It was so big it was grotesque. It was ugly. Why was Nelson always bragging about the tree—like it was worth a million bucks? It didn't grow dollar bills. It just stood there.

"Who needs it?" Craig said.

He plunged through the underbrush until he emerged from the woods. He headed straight for the tool shed—a small wooden building which had been part of the original plantation. Craig had been in there many times. He knew where to find the chain saw. When he hefted the saw from its shelf, it felt light.

"Needs gas."

Craig filled the gas well from the can under the table, carelessly splashing gas on the floor.

The saw was heavier now, but flowing adrenalin gave him power. He carried the saw over to the tree. He pulled the cord once. Twice. The engine sputtered. He pulled again, harder, and the machine started. Holding the saw with both hands, Craig looked up at the tree. He bunched his muscles and steeled himself.

"You're coming down!" Craig lunged at the tree.

When the blade first touched the trunk of the tree it

glanced off. The shock of it sent Craig back a step or two. He gripped harder and started again. The blade ate into the bark of the tree and stuck there. Craig wrenched it free. That killed the motor, so Craig had to start it again. It wasn't going to be easy to fell this giant.

Craig planted his feet firmly and bent to the task. He grunted like an animal, and the saw bit into the tree once more. This time Craig didn't try to cut straight through the tree.

The saw slid sideways into the wood. Craig took a step to his right and the saw blade moved, too. Grunting and yelling, bent over with the saw vibrating through his hands and arms, Craig slowly walked around the tree, slicing a deep cut into the bark.

By the time Craig circled the tree almost back to where he started, he knew he would never be able to cut it down. The saw smoked and shuttered because Craig had been in such a hurry he hadn't mixed oil with the gasoline. He was crying now. The weight and jarring of the saw deadened his arms. A part of him was still filled with hate and anger and arrogance—it was like those other times—he didn't care what anybody thought. He would do what he damn well pleased. But, another part of him was amazed at himself. Why was he doing this? The Arks had always been good to him. They never hurt him in any way. They didn't beat him or make him poor, and they weren't responsible for his mother's death. Why was he taking his frustrations out on them?

Blinded by tears, Craig didn't see the tree root

spreading out from the base of the tree, six inches or so above the ground.

When he stumbled over the root, Craig knew he was in trouble. As he pitched forward, he tried to hold onto the saw long enough to throw it a safe distance away. But it caught on the rope of the ladder and was wrenched from his hands. Craig landed on his stomach, arms stretched out, and the saw flipped over his back and came down, buzzing.

Craig screamed as the teeth of the saw cut though the top of his boot and into his leg. The tough leather was too much for the stressed saw; it sputtered and jerked to a stop. Pain and blackness closed in on Craig's mind.

Chapter Two

*"Hurt not the earth,
neither the sea, nor the trees."*
THE BIBLE, Revelation

Slowly, Craig came back from a dark faraway place, his eyes still closed. He smelled the dust of dry leaves. Hard earth cradled his cheek. He smiled because his mother was washing his face with a wet wash cloth. But, how could that be? She was... Craig opened his eyes and looked into Siegfried's face. The rough wash cloth was Siegfried's tongue. What happened?

As he tried to raise himself, Craig became aware of sounds—the voices of Mrs. Ark and Nelson. He groaned and slumped back onto the ground.

"Here, Siegfried," called Nelson.

"Don't touch that saw, Nelson," Mrs. Ark said. "I'll lift it off him."

The chain saw. Now Craig remembered. The tree. He had done a terrible thing. He wished he could stay unconscious or melt into the earth, but the pain in his leg wouldn't let him.

"Are you all right, Craig?" Mrs. Ark asked. "Lie still." Craig heard a ripping sound as Mrs. Ark tore an even bigger hole in his jeans. He moaned when she pulled off the slashed boot.

"Oh, dear," murmured Mrs. Ark. "We need to stop the blood." Mrs. Ark took off her sweat suit jacket and wrapped it tightly around the bleeding leg.

"Look what he did, Mom!" Nelson walked all the way around the tree. "What is the matter with you, Craig?" he shouted. "Have you gone crazy? I don't get this! Why—?" His mother interrupted the tirade.

"We'll worry about that later, Nelson. For now, let's take him to the emergency room. We need to hurry. Help me get him into the car." Mrs. Ark's usual calm voice trembled with anxiety. "Turn over and sit up, Craig. We can get you to Dr. Leopold quicker than the ambulance can get here." She and Nelson helped Craig to stand and with some difficulty got him into the car. Siegfried scurried back and forth between the group and the car barking.

Craig looked straight ahead to avoid the puzzled expressions on the faces of Nelson and Mrs. Ark. Not that it mattered; he knew they didn't want to look at him, either.

Siegfried jumped in to sit with Craig in the back of the car. Nelson got into the front seat beside his mother and they drove off.

"I'll go as fast as I can," Mrs. Ark said.

The grim trip to the small town of Magnolia Crest was shrouded in silence, each person in the car detached from the others. His own actions baffled Craig. *Mrs. Ark and Nelson are wondering what got into me.* It was a big deal, he knew, and that made the stillness frightening, like being in the eye of a storm. Something terrible lurked on the other side of this hush. Each time a low moan escaped Craig, Siegfried, his head in Craig's lap, answered with a sympathetic whimper.

The light of day was fading, and Craig felt the darkness envelop his life as evening enveloped the car. The glow of windows in the sparsely scattered houses leading to town made Craig feel like a mariner adrift on a leaden sea.

Mrs. Ark sighed. "Ohh...Nelson, what was all the commotion about as you were leaving the K'BeTs meeting?" She slowed the car down, now they were in town.

Looks like she doesn't want to talk about me. Craig shrugged.

"Some of the kids were fussing about our next service project. Shaquan wants to build a skateboard ramp at the town park. But Carson suggested we fix up old toys for needy kids. She thinks building a skateboard ramp is selfish of us."

"What do you want to do?"

"I haven't decided," Nelson said.

Mrs. Ark turned into the emergency room parking lot, so they said no more about the service project.

The emergency room was housed in a small brick building surrounded by trees and azalea bushes. A sign pointed to an ambulance entrance around back. Craig wondered if he would be taken to the hospital in the city. A few parking spaces were lined up along the driveway, facing the street. After parking the car, Mrs. Ark sent Nelson into the ER for a wheelchair. They helped Craig into the chair.

"I left the car windows rolled down a few inches for

Siegfried," Mrs. Ark said, as she helped Nelson push the wheelchair into the building.

It took only a few minutes for Mrs. Ark to explain what happened. The receptionist checked Craig into the emergency room and then the nurse, Mrs. Chandler, took over. The ER was a small, two-room setup with a few chairs in the hall opposite the treatment cubicles.

"I'll get the doctor," said the receptionist.

As the nurse wheeled Craig away, Mrs. Ark called, "We'll be right here, Craig."

Somehow, that made him feel a little better.

The doctor closed the curtain as he entered the cubicle to examine Craig. "What have we here, Craig?" His tone was full of soothing concern.

"I hurt my leg."

"Well, let's see if we can fix you up, young man." Craig remembered Dr. Leopold's kindly voice and friendly eyes from the time he treated Craig's mother.

"Mrs. Chandler, let's give Craig a tetanus shot and pill to make him drowsy."

The nurse gave Craig the pill and the injection and helped him take off his jeans and the other boot. Craig lay face down on the examining table. He flinched as Mrs. Chandler cleaned the wound and gave him a shot of something to numb the area while the doctor sewed up the torn muscle and skin.

"You're fortunate there was no major blood vessel cut, Craig." Dr. Leopold laid his hand on Craig's shoulder. "It's 'a flesh wound,' as they used to say in the old western movies.

Wounds

But, what about these other bruises and scars? Not all of these are fresh." Addressing the nurse, he said, "Help Craig off with his shirt, Mrs. Chandler."

Under the effect of the sedative Craig had no will to refuse, even though he didn't want to expose all of his wounds to the world. He did as the doctor wanted. He sat up and took off his shirt. He heard the nurse stifle a quick intake of breath when she saw Craig's torso. The doctor peered at Craig's bruised eye and swollen lip encrusted with dried blood.

"Craig, did you hurt your face when you hurt your leg?"

Craig said nothing. He turned away from the doctor and lay back on the table.

"Look after him, Mrs. Chandler," said the doctor, "and clean him up. He needs an ice pack for his face and some rest."

Craig closed his eyes and listened to the doctor slide the curtain aside and step into the hall. Craig was vaguely aware of Mrs. Ark and Nelson talking while he was being cared for. Now, while the nurse worked quietly, he tuned in to what was being said in the waiting area outside his cubicle.

"We have a puzzling situation here, Lisa," the doctor said. "I'm very concerned. This boy is more beat up than a prize fighter."

"He hurt his leg when he attacked our old oak with a chain saw—you know the one. I don't have any idea what made him do such a thing." Mrs. Ark did sound puzzled. "I don't know what else could have happened to him, Douglas."

13

"He has some fresh wounds aside from the cut on his leg—his black eye and swollen lip, which I'm sure you saw."

"Yes, but I assumed that happened when he hurt his leg; he fell face down."

"He wouldn't tell me how he got those injuries. And in addition to them, he has several bruises and scars over his body and limbs."

"I don't know what has been happening to him. He doesn't come to our house since Julia died." After a pause, Mrs. Ark asked, "Do you know anything about any accident Craig had, Nelson?"

Craig was glad he could hold the ice pack over his face. He lay quietly while the nurse tiptoed out of the cubicle.

"Not really," Craig heard Nelson answer his mother's question. "I don't keep up with Craig now. We haven't been friends this year. We don't even sit together on the school bus anymore. He just isn't friendly. But he did miss a few days of school last month. I heard he had a broken rib."

"If so, he didn't come to see me with it," Dr. Leopold said. "Well, if you will excuse me, I have a telephone call to make."

Craig heard the doctor's steps fade away.

Nelson spoke in a lowered tone. "And, Mom, he's been in trouble a few times at school. He had detention for messing up the art teacher's bulletin board. It made a lot of the kids mad. And he wrote on the math teacher's car with a permanent marker. Stuff like that."

Craig cringed when he heard his former friend say

those things. *You don't know, Nelson. You just don't know.*
Still it hurt.

Chapter Three

> *"Woodman, spare that tree!*
> *Touch not a single bough.*
> *In youth it sheltered me*
> *And I'll protect it now."*
> George Pope Morris

The front door of the emergency room opened. Someone burst in and demanded angrily, "What's going on, Lisa?" From inside his cubicle, Craig recognized Mr. Ark's voice.

"What's this about the tree? Did Craig actually try to cut it down?"

"I don't know what Craig was trying to do, Bentley. But what's done is done. Now you must try to keep calm. Why don't you sit down and wait for Charlie to arrive. I've been trying to get him on the phone."

Craig heard Mr. Ark's footsteps. Knowing Mr. Ark, he couldn't sit down and get calm. He was probably running his hand through his hair in an act of frustration, as he did when situations were out of his control, like last year when the hurricane destroyed a lot of his carpet store.

"This is incredible." Mr. Ark's voice trembled. "Unthinkable. What got into him? I'd like to shake an explanation out of him. When can I talk to him?" Each time he came near Craig's cubicle, Craig recoiled at the sound of Mr.

16

Ark's voice, alternately gruff and despondent.

Dr. Leopold came out of his office. "I'm sorry to hear about the old tree, Bentley, but we have an even bigger problem. It looks to me as if the boy has been beaten—and more than once. I suspect it was his dad."

"I knew Charlie was dejected ever since Julia died, but I never dreamed he would beat the boy." Mr. Ark let out a loud sigh and asked, "What are you going to do about it?"

"I had to report it to the state authorities. I just called the hot line in Tallahassee. They're sending a social worker here. Probably Marjorie Dayton."

"Well, I'm calling the police." Mr. Ark didn't shout, but his tone was forceful. "This business with the tree is more than I can take. Somebody is going to pay."

"Now, Bentley..." Mrs. Ark started in her gentle way.

He wouldn't let her finish. "I mean it, Lisa. I'm not saying I want Craig sent to jail. Charlie's the one who's really responsible. And I mean to see he pays." Then, more calmly he said, "Please hand me your cellphone; I must have left mine in the car."

Craig heard Mr. Ark phone the sheriff's office. "Rod Boyle will be here soon." For a moment, no one said anything.

Lying alone in his little room, Craig listened to his situation grow worse. *Oh, great; not only did I not escape, now I'll be going to jail.*

"Nelson," said Mrs. Ark, "run out to the car and take Siegfried for a little walk, honey."

"Okay, Mom."

"Give me the phone back, Bentley, before you squeeze it in two. I'll try again to locate Charlie. I can't think where he would be at this time of evening. The last I heard he didn't have a job. Maybe he's home now." She made the call again and said, "It keeps ringing; there isn't an answering machine. Douglas, may I stay with Craig until his father gets here?"

"Why, sure, Lisa," said the doctor. "I'll be in my office if you need me."

Mrs. Ark joined Craig behind the curtain.

"Are you awake, Craig? Can I do anything for you?"

"No."

Craig wanted to tell Mrs. Ark he appreciated her being there, but he felt ashamed at betraying her friendship. He kept his eyes shut and a scowl on his face; now he had proved himself to be a bad kid he might as well stick with it.

The outer door opened and closed, and Craig heard Nelson say, "Siegfried is fine."

"I am just heartsick." Mr. Ark's voice came through the curtain. His voice clawed itself over broken glass. "That tree is like a member of the family. Do you feel that way about it, Nelson?"

"Yeah," said Nelson. "It's a great place to play. It's better than a jungle gym."

Craig stole a glance at Mrs. Ark. She turned away from him and busied herself by folding and refolding his clothes. Craig covered his face with the ice pack.

"I remember when I was a boy," Mr. Ark said, his voice wistful. "I played in it just the way you do. And my dad told me he had, also. My dad told me a lot about the tree. In fact," he said with some enthusiasm, "he told me about a time when the tree was attacked by gypsy moths. The moth caterpillars nearly stripped it of its leaves. Then the leaves grew right back. Live oaks have a strong immune system. The tree is robust. I think it will be okay."

Craig heard the hope in Mr. Ark's voice. With his eyes closed, Craig lay listening to Mr. Ark and Nelson talk about the tree. Separated from him by the curtain, it seemed Craig and Mr. Ark were joined by the tree. As Mr. Ark talked, Craig lived the life of the tree.

"Why, you know, Nelson, the tree has bullet holes and arrow holes that have healed over so you can barely see them. An important treaty of the Seminole Wars was signed under the old oak. It was considered a sacred place by the Indians."

Nelson said, "I guess they thought anybody who made an agreement under that tree would be bound to keep it."

"I guess," said Mr. Ark. "Then later, spies from both the Yankee and Rebel armies hid up in the tree from time to time to gather information about the enemy, and wounded soldiers lay on stretchers in the shade of the tree getting stitched up."

"And how about the Ponce de Leon legend?" Nelson joined in his dad's enthusiasm.

"They say he poured a flask of water from the Fountain of Youth right on the tree. Of course, at the time, it was only a sapling."

"Well, maybe that's why it's lived so long and been so

healthy," said Nelson.

"Maybe…" Mr. Ark laughed. "However, I'm not sure Ponce de Leon ever got this far west; it could just be big talk."

Craig could see the images of the tree as Mr. Ark created them.

"Several beautiful brides have celebrated their weddings there—your mother was one of them and so was mine. My granddaddy used a piece of a broken limb to carve a Noah's ark set for my grandmother. That was the beginning of the ark collection. Then my daddy made the curio cabinet to display the whole bunch… It has a noble history—our tree."

All this concern about a tree. Was this the biggest problem the Ark family had? Craig wondered.

Mr. Ark started pacing the floor again. It seemed as if his thoughts had come full circle. "But, we'll have to wait and see. Did you say he went all the way around the tree?"

"Just about," Nelson said. "I walked around it. The cut was all but about two feet around."

"But how deep was it?" asked his dad. "That's the important thing. Did it go below the bark?"

"It didn't look so deep to me, in most places," Nelson said. "About an inch, or maybe half an inch. Why is that important? There's no way Craig could cut that big tree down."

A groan of despair escaped Mr. Ark. "Ohhhhhhh!"

"What's wrong, Dad?" Nelson sounded worried. "Are you sick?"

"It's not me, son," Mr. Ark said. "It's the tree I'm

thinking about. If the cut goes beneath the bark into the living part of the tree then the tree is in real trouble."

"Why is that?" Nelson asked.

"What I mean is, well—the bark is like armor—it isn't the living part of the tree. The tissue under the bark is where the tree grows. It's where the sap runs and the tree gets fed."

"Dad, I know the tree means a lot to you, to me too, and Mom. Well, maybe it can be fixed. Isn't there something you could do?"

"You're right, Nelson." Hope won another battle in the war with despair. "I'll call in a tree surgeon. We'll spare no expense. That tree is worth every effort it will take to save it!"

Chapter Four

> *". . . their fruit will be for food,*
> *and their leaves for healing."*
> THE BIBLE, Ezekiel 47:12

Craig stirred on the narrow bed.

"Are you feeling any better, Craig?" Mrs. Ark said.

"My leg hurts," he replied. "What time is it? Did I fall asleep?"

"Yes, you did. It's about eight-thirty. While you were napping, my husband went out for food. Here's a burger and a shake for you." She smiled. "He even got one for Siegfried." She brought over a little rolling table with the food on it.

"I don't want it." The smell made Craig queasy.

"You need to build up your strength; there are some people here to talk to you."

"I don't want to see anybody." Craig heard people talking in the hall; a woman and a man had joined the doctor and Mr. Ark. The voice he dreaded to hear was not there—his father's.

"Craig," Mrs. Ark said, "these people are here to help you. They're going to take charge whether you cooperate or not. I hope you'll let them do their jobs."

Craig knew Mrs. Ark wanted to help him. She was always doing nice things for him. He liked her, but he couldn't show that now; he had to hang tough.

"Who's out there? Where's my dad?" Craig felt a flutter of nerves in the middle of his body.

"I don't know where your dad is. We've been trying to find him. Deputy Boyle is here and so is a social worker, Mrs. Dayton. They're going to need information from you. Shall I call them in now?"

Craig let out a sigh. His dejection and hopelessness came out in surly tones. "What the heck; let's get it over with." He was weary of the whole affair; he wished he could sleep for a month—maybe he could sleep for twenty years like Rip Van Winkle. How else could he get out of this jam?

Mrs. Ark pushed aside the curtain and invited the officials into Craig's cubicle. She retrieved her bloody sweat suit jacket and stepped out.

Craig really felt abandoned now. The memory of a dream came to him. He pictured the giant oak alone on a vast plain—no, it was more like a lifeless desert. It, too, felt lonely. Isolated. Abandoned. He quickly shut out the image.

His room filled with authority figures. Craig allowed the doctor to help him into a sitting position on the bed, his bandaged leg propped on a stool, and submitted to the questioning. Did he know where his father might have gone? Did he have any relatives in the area who would take him in if his father could not be found? Where did he get the bruises and scars? Were they inflicted by his father?

Craig was unwilling to look at his inquisitors. He was as withdrawn and sulky as he felt he could get away with. He hated the fact he couldn't keep his face from burning when he admitted his dad beat him. By the end of Craig's story, the whole ugly mess tumbled out for the officials to picture scenes of drunken fury and abuse. Only the most important things Craig did not tell.

"Craig," Dr. Leopold asked, "did your dad break one of your ribs?"

"Yeah."

"Why didn't you come to me?"

Craig looked squarely at the doctor. At last, he was able to put some pride into his voice. "It got okay by itself."

The doctor looked at Mrs. Dayton, who returned his look with upraised eyebrows. Craig saw the silent message.

Presently, the receptionist called the deputy into the hall. He returned in a few moments, shaking his head and wrinkling his brow. He blew out a breath of air and said, "Deputy Stoneman just returned from the Reeves house. There was no sign of Charlie. We've checked with most of his known hangouts. Looks like he's run away."

"In that case," Mrs. Dayton said, "I'll take Craig to Family Services' temporary shelter. He can stay there at least three nights. You do what you have to, Rod. Let me know when you locate Mr. Reeves."

"Will do." Deputy Boyle saluted smartly and left the emergency room.

Turning to the doctor, Mrs. Dayton asked, "Is Craig well enough to go with me to Juvenile Justice tomorrow?"

"If he favors the injured leg and uses crutches, he

should be able to go. Just bring him back for a checkup within forty-eight hours. Here's some pain medication for you to take to the shelter."

"Thank you, Dr. Leopold." Mrs. Dayton put the bottle in her purse.

The doctor called the nurse to help Craig back into his clothes—the jeans torn and stiff with blood. As Craig limped out of the emergency room on his crutches, he passed the Ark family.

Nelson raised his hand in front of his chest and said quietly, "See ya, Craig."

Mrs. Ark clutched the bloody sweat suit jacket and smiled weakly. Mr. Ark, his back turned, leaned on the reception desk, slumped like a strong tree buffeted by fierce winds.

Mrs. Dayton took Craig by the arm. "Let's get you over to Hope House, Craig," she said, in a forced cheerful voice, "and set you up in the system."

Craig heard Mrs. Ark gasp. He turned and saw her grab her husband's arm. "Oh, Bentley," she said, "he will be lost."

The last thing Craig heard as he made his way slowly out the door was spoken by Nelson: "Dad, would it be worth every effort to save a boy?"

Chapter Five

> *"Cut is the*
> *branch that might have*
> *Grown full straight."*
> Christopher Marlow
> THE TRAGICAL HISTORY OF
> DOCTOR FAUSTUS

Mrs. Dayton stopped the van in front of an ordinary looking two-story white house. Craig looked up. "It doesn't have a fence." Then again, neither did Camp Greenlake in *Holes*.

"No," Mrs. Dayton said, cheerily, "but the doors are kept locked; you'll be safe here."

"Don't you mean it'll be impossible for me to escape?"

"Now why would you want to leave this place? Your dad can't get to you and Mrs. Hudson is an excellent cook." She took off her glasses and pressed the bridge of her nose with her thumb and forefinger. "Mr. and Mrs. Hudson will take very good care of you, Craig. And remember, it's only for a few nights." She replaced the glasses and got out of the van.

Craig felt very tired and the challenge went out of him. All he wanted was to be let alone.

Mrs. Dayton helped Craig out of the van and up the

steps by the yellow beams of a lantern-style porch light. He struggled to balance on the crutches.

Mrs. Dayton rang the doorbell, and the door was opened by a round woman with a smiling moon face and wisps of salt and pepper hair escaping from a forest of bobby pins. "We bin expectin' you…" Mrs. Hudson said in her sing-song voice. "Come on in, Mrs. Dayton, and this is Craig, ain't it?" Mrs. Hudson enfolded Craig in a welcoming hug, but he stiffened and jerked his head aside.

"Craig, this is Mrs. Hudson." Mrs. Dayton spoke slowly and deliberately.

Only somewhat defiant, Craig simply grunted, "Hello."

The ladies made Craig comfortable on a hall chair while they went into the office to the left of the entrance to finish the business of settling Craig into Hope House.

Sitting with ears straining, Craig overheard the conversation in the office which made his ears burn. "…out of control; tearing things up at school."…"What a pity."…"That type of vandalism can quickly develop into hurting animals and then people."…"Don't I know. Honey, I seen ter-ble things go on with some of these kids. The things I could tell you."…"Well, never mind that now. Here's Craig's pain medication. I'll be back early in the morning to pick him up."

Craig heard a faint rustle which broke his attention. He looked up to catch a glimpse of a young girl with spindly legs. She sneaked through the dining room, which was opposite the office, toward the back of the house. *I wonder how many other kids are here. I hope it's just that one.*

He found out soon enough. After Mrs. Dayton left, wishing him a restful night and telling him she would pick him up at ten in the morning, Mrs. Hudson locked the door and said, "You're hungry, ain't you, Craig? Come on to the kitchen and have a bite and meet the rest of the family."

Mrs. Hudson led the way down the hall, not through the dining room. "You need plenty of room to navigate with them crutches, don't you, Craig?"

Craig followed her unsmiling to the kitchen. There was an old man of about fifty, Craig guessed, with a stubble of end-of-the-day beard, wearing denims and a flowered necktie with a plaid shirt. *Even I have better taste than that,* thought Craig, wishing his best baggy jeans hadn't gotten torn up.

"This is Mr. Hudson, Craig," said Mrs. Hudson, introducing him to her husband. "And you can call me Miz Frannie. Kids have been calling me that many a year, ain't they, now?"

Mr. Hudson offered his hand to Craig, but Craig pretended the crutches took all his attention. Mr. Hudson withdrew his hand and said, "Glad to have you here with us, Craig. D'ya have any belongings for me to take upstairs?"

"No," mumbled Craig. Then in a pang of conscience, he added, "Sir."

"Never you mind," said Miz Frannie. "We have plenty of clothes for a boy your age. About fourteen, are you?" she added.

"I'm thirteen," said Craig.

"My, you're big for your age, ain't you?" Miz Frannie

disappeared to get a supply of clothes for Craig, muttering, "Large boy size."

When she returned with an armload of clothes and toiletries, she offered Craig some leftovers from dinner.

"I'm not hungry," he said. "Somebody bought me a hamburger." He failed to tell her he hadn't eaten that either. He really wasn't hungry. He felt a little sick to his stomach, but the emptiness he felt was not in his body. Since his mother died and his dad changed so much, emptiness gnawed at his heart. It set him apart and engulfed him. He felt like the guy in that movie—the one in the bubble. He couldn't touch anyone, and no one could touch him… Except there were times when he burst out. What made it bad was being out of control at those times. Instead of touching people, he hurt them. Is that what Mrs. Dayton had been talking about? But at least, then, he was not cut off.

Miz Frannie persuaded Craig to drink a glass of milk. "It will help to settle your stomach, don't you think?" she said, brushing hair out of her eyes with the back of her hand.

While Craig drank his milk, Miz Frannie called two girls into the kitchen, one about ten, the other about seven. The smaller clung to Mrs. Hudson like ivy. Her face was tear-streaked and the front of her dress was wet. She was in no shape to be sociable. And though Miz Frannie hugged her and wiped her face with tissues and made comforting sounds, the girl remained inconsolable.

"When's my mommy coming to get me?" was all she would say.

The other girl looked at her with disdain and rolled her eyes. She was the girl Craig had seen scuttering away earlier. The spy moved like a caged animal, her brown eyes darting this way and that, the fingers of her right hand pinching and picking at the reddened skin of the left. It made Craig think of what he read about trapped animals chewing off their own legs to escape the snare.

Mr. Hudson brought the other tenant from the TV room. "I don't want to miss my show," the boy whined.

"Hush, now," said Mr. Hudson, "and come on meet the new boy."

The boy dragged himself reluctantly into the kitchen. He was about Craig's height, but thinner. The insolent expression in his eyes spoke of experiences that had aged him.

The boys said, "Hi," to each other and resumed their various activities.

Miz Frannie continued to be cheerful. Although she seemed sincere, Craig wondered if she wasn't trying too hard to make this all seem natural and normal. But looking at the drawn, tense faces of the children in her care, Craig knew it was just the opposite.

When Miz Frannie put the girls to bed upstairs, Mr. Hudson led the boys up to the room they would share. "Now, Craig," said Mr. Hudson, "we all try to help each other here. We have lights out at ten o'clock on weekends and nine on school nights. Eat all you want at meals but don't waste. And no fussin' or fightin.' And use the tooth brush Miz Frannie gave you."

"Yeah, sure," said Craig, as he propped his crutches against a chair and lowered himself onto the bed.

Craig welcomed the pain reliever Dr. Leopold sent over with Mrs. Dayton. Miz Frannie gave him water with which to swallow the pills. She hugged both boys before putting out the light and closing the door.

"Got a smoke on you?" Craig heard in the darkness.

"What do you mean?"

"A smoke. A fag. Have you got any cigarettes?" The boy spoke with impatience.

"No," Craig said, "I don't smoke."

"Oh, hell! That's great. No smoke, no video games, and I gotta listen to that brat across the hall crying for her mother. Her mother ain't coming. She otta know by now. She's being shipped off to another foster home tomorrow."

"What do you mean 'another'?" Craig asked.

"I've seen her here before. They never keep her for long; they can't do nothing with her. She's 'uncooperative.'"

"How many times have you been here?" Craig wondered if this kid had also been labeled "uncooperative."

"Enough. Mind your own business."

That silenced Craig, but a few minutes later his roommate said, "How about money? You got any cash?"

"No."

"If you're still here on Monday, the ole lady will give you a backpack for school. I can tell you where you can sell it for the most money. Then just tell her you lost it. Tomorrow I'll show you how to play craps." The boy's voice went from conspiratorial to bragging. "I can get you a pair of dice that will never fail you. You can rip off any sucker stupid enough to get into a game with you. I'm gonna be a big man some day. I know some important people. I got it all planned out. Stick with me, man. We'll be rich by the time we're twenty."

"Thanks, but, no thanks," said Craig. He could just imagine where this dude would be in seven years. Talk about a lost boy; Mrs. Ark should get a load of him. Craig wanted no part of this loser. He wanted no part of this place—ever again. Though he sure didn't want to return home to his dad, even that seemed better than the revolving-door nightmare these other kids were spinning in. He wanted things to be the way they used to be. What was going to happen to him?

The red tip-end of a cigarette glowed in the dark. "Found a fag and a match," said the boy.

"The smell of brimstone," muttered Craig.

"Come over here and watch me sizzle this palmetto bug."

"That's gross." *Was this guy nuts?*

The bedroom door opened and Craig saw Mr. Hudson outlined in the doorway. "Let me have that cigarette. You know smoking is not allowed here."

The boy didn't protest and Mr. Hudson left after putting the fire out in a dish on the dresser. "Good night, boys," he said amiably.

"The ole fool," hissed the boy.

Craig turned to the wall, but though exhausted, he couldn't sleep. Unbidden, the events of the day pushed themselves into Craig's mind, and each time, he pushed them out. He lay listening to the night sounds of the shelter. After everyone else seemed to be asleep, Craig heard the little girl across the hall sobbing for her mother. Another abandoned kid.

Soon sleep immersed Craig in dreams of skeletal trees menacing terrified lost boys. This was not the imaginary world of Peter Pan; his Neverland was real.

Chapter Six

*"There was an old owl liv'd in an oak,
The more he heard, the less he spoke,
The less he spoke, the more he heard,
O, if men were all like that wise bird."*
PUNCH

As she promised, Mrs. Dayton picked Craig up at ten o'clock Friday morning to go to juvenile court.

It had been hard for Craig to wake up. Before a small breakfast, he washed and dressed in the odd assortment of clothes Miz Frannie provided. "Let's throw these old boots away, what do ya say?" she said. "I got some better ones for you."

"It's okay with me," Craig said. "They were hand-me-downs anyway."

Miz Frannie also changed the dressing on his wound.

While Craig waited for Mrs. Dayton, the forlorn trio waited for foster parents. The spy skulked, the crybaby cried, and the lost boy tried to interest Craig in a game of craps. But Craig brushed him off. Even though Craig was apprehensive about going to court, he was glad to see Mrs. Dayton. As soon as they were in the van, he asked her if his dad would be at the courthouse.

"No, Craig, he hasn't been found yet; the sheriff is still

looking. And even if he is found," she released a heavy sigh, "you might not be permitted to go home with him."

"I don't want to go home with him! Why do you think I ran away yesterday? I want to be on my own."

"Craig, you know that is unrealistic. The state can't permit it. Now you mustn't worry. Even if your dad can't or won't live up to his responsibilities, someone will take care of you."

"Yeah, I heard all about those foster homes. Those kids at Hope House are all miserable; you should call it 'Hopeless House.'"

"Craig, don't become cynical. Not all foster situations are the same."

"Yeah, I'll bet."

Craig grew more and more nervous as they drove to the county seat ten miles from Magnolia Crest. By the time they entered the courtroom, his palms were sweating. He felt his facial muscles involuntarily contort into a silly grin. He felt really stupid. He was so jittery he lurched on his crutches and almost fell on the oiled wooden floor.

Mrs. Dayton led Craig into a small room. That was a relief; large courtrooms were for criminals. The judge was about the age Craig's grandfathers would be if they had lived. He was dressed as Craig expected, in a black robe. He wore glasses and had thinning gray hair. Craig and Mrs. Dayton sat at a table facing the judge, and Deputy Boyle sat at a table beside theirs.

"This is Judge Borowsky, Craig," Mrs. Dayton

whispered.

Mrs. Dayton explained Craig's situation to the court and what happened the day before. The deputy informed the judge the boy's father had not been located. After inquiring of the neighbors, he ascertained there were no relatives in the area.

"I see there are two issues to deal with," Judge Borowsky said in a deep, slow drawl, "but this hearing cannot concern itself with the vandalism. We will proceed to deal with the welfare of this minor. Mrs. Dayton, as an officer of the Department of Family Services, do you have a recommendation for placement of this boy?"

"There is a very fine family who has recently requested…"

Craig listened quietly while the officials talked about him almost as if he were a thing. A rushing wind began to blow inside his head and he felt far away. He could no longer hear what Mrs. Dayton was saying. Where was his dad? Why had his dad run away? Why didn't he come and rescue Craig? Craig's breathing became slow and deep. His shoulders and chest were rising. His face felt hot and his hands were shaking. He tried to speak, but his mouth trembled. His breath was now coming in quick jerks. He forced out the words.

"I don't want to live with strangers!"

"He's hyperventilating, Your Honor," said Mrs. Dayton. "Slow down your breathing, Craig," she said, as she patted him on the shoulder. "Calm yourself. Put your head down on the table."

With his head resting on his crossed forearms, Craig managed to slow his breathing. When the judge's assistant brought him a glass of water, he straightened up. Aided by Mrs. Dayton, Craig brought the glass to his lips with shaking hands and took a sip of water. After a few minutes he didn't feel so jittery. The courtroom remained quiet while Craig composed himself.

"Are you feeling better, Craig?" asked Mrs. Dayton.

"Yes," he replied.

Presently Judge Borowsky said, "Craig, you must trust us. We will do what is best for you. Mrs. Dayton will find a good foster home for you until we can be sure your father can provide you with the stability you need."

"Your Honor," Mrs. Dayton said, "I will need to return Craig to Mr. and Mrs. Hudson until I can arrange a suitable home for him."

Craig's panic began to recede, but he wished he could forget those kids at the shelter. He turned imploring eyes on Mrs. Dayton.

The social worker looked at the judge, who was speaking to her. "Mrs. Dayton, I will permit the Division of Family Services to place—"

The judge's words were cut off by a knock on the courtroom door. The policeman at the door opened it and admitted Mr. Bentley Ark.

"I'm sorry to interrupt, Judge Borowsky," Mr. Ark said, to the now scowling judge, "but may I be allowed to speak?"

"This is highly irregular, Mr. Ark," the judge said. "I believe your concern in this situation involves Mr. Reeves, not the boy. The problem of the tree is a criminal action which is not the purpose of today's proceedings."

"I realize that, Judge Borowsky." Mr. Ark appeared to stand taller. "I'm not here about the tree… I'm here to ask for custody of Craig."

The room became hushed after a sharp intake of breath from Craig. *Now I'll catch it. He'll beat me for cutting his old tree.*

Mrs. Dayton stood up and placed her hands protectively on Craig's shoulders.

Deputy Boyle was the first of the astonished audience to respond. "Are you planning to take the tree's price out o' Craig's hide, Bentley?"

"No, of course not, Rod," said Mr. Ark, spreading his empty hands out at his sides. "I've talked this over very carefully with my wife and son. We've known Craig a long time and he isn't a bad kid—really. We could have done a whole lot more for him after his mother died than we did. We had troubles of our own at the time, so we didn't know how bad his home life had gotten."

"But, Bentley," said Deputy Boyle, "you were mad as heck last night."

"Yes, I was. I was furious," said Mr. Ark, "and I'm still heartsick about the tree. But, weighed in the balance, the life of a boy outweighs that of a tree. If I can't save the tree, maybe I can at least save the boy."

Craig looked around at the people in the courtroom. They looked as puzzled as he felt. But Craig knew he was the most stunned of all. When he looked at Mr. Ark their gaze met and locked. With the specter of the tree hovering between them, Craig saw a co-mingling of intense pain and tenderness on Mr. Ark's face.

How could I go live with him? I'm his worst enemy.

"Your Honor," said Mr. Ark, "my wife and I don't want Craig to get into the state system; nor do we want him returned to his father—at least not yet."

"Let me get this straight, Mr. Ark." Judge Borosky's gaze bored into Mr. Ark's eyes. "You are offering your home to the vandal who tried to destroy one of your most prized possessions?"

"I know it's bizarre, Your Honor. Now, don't get me wrong. I'm no Goody Two-Shoes. This is just common sense. I don't want to put this boy in a place where he can learn to become a real criminal."

"Oh, I suspect there's more than common sense at play here…but we're not sending him to prison, Mr. Ark."

"Yes, sir. Nevertheless, the foster home circuit is simply unnecessary in this case. Why burden the state and place the child with strangers, when there is a family he knows who will take him in?"

Craig sat quietly while this exchange took place. Mrs. Dayton resumed her seat beside him, perched on the edge of her chair. Mr. Ark inched closer to the judge's table.

Judge Borowsky took off his glasses and swiveled his

chair toward the window. No one said a word while the judge sat in deep concentration.

Craig lost his sense of time. He did not know if a second or an eternity passed while the judge decided his future.

Turning back around, the judge swiped his hand across his mouth. Craig saw him grimace. Or was it a smile he was trying to conceal? A grimace didn't jibe with the twinkle in Judge Borowsky's eyes. Replacing his glasses, the judge straightened his face and looked at Mr. Ark.

"I have tried to give a measure of thoughtful consideration to your proposal, Mr. Ark. And now that I think it over," the judge was really smiling now, "this may be the perfect solution. Perfect for both issues. As I said earlier, the criminal charges will have to be taken against the father. But in the meantime, we can provide the boy with a good home and exact some recompense for the damage he has done. However, Mr. Ark," continued the judge in a more business-like tone, "the boy is still the ward of the state. Even if he goes with you, the arrangements will have to be made by Mrs. Dayton."

"I understand, Your Honor." Mr. Ark nodded his head.

The judge turned from Mr. Ark and addressed Craig. "Craig, Mr. Ark is not going to hurt you, or punish you. I have known him since he was knee-high to a jack-rabbit, and he may be a little excitable, but he is an honorable man. His father and I were old fishing buddies. Now, he is offering you a good home. And I'm going to give you an opportunity to make amends for your poor behavior."

Craig didn't know if he was supposed to respond to the judge, so he waited to be prompted. He wondered what the judge meant by "amends." *Am I supposed to mend the tree?*

Judge Borosky's face took on a serious expression. "Craig, you have done a deplorable thing. I want you to consider what you have done. And I want you to be helpful to Mr. and Mrs. Ark. There's nothing like hard work to straighten out confused thinking."

So Craig was delivered from living with strangers, or worse, going to prison. But why should he let the judge see his relief? "Yes, sir," he said, looking down at his hands. *I'll go for now; I'm so tired, I need a place to crash.*

The judge addressed the social worker. "Mrs. Dayton, do you have anything to add to this settlement?"

"No, Your Honor," she said, smiling. "It sounds like a plan to me. I'll take care of the red tape, uh, that is, the paperwork."

For once, Craig thought, she sounded sincerely pleased.

"Therefore, Craig," Judge Borowsky said, "I hereby sentence you to live in a comfortable, loving home and be the caretaker of the Venerable Old Oak."

The rest of the hearing passed quickly and in a haze for Craig. All of the adults seemed happy with his new arrangement. Mrs. Dayton said she would keep the court apprised of Craig's progress. Deputy Boyle said the sheriff's office would continue the search for Mr. Reeves; he didn't think it would take long to find him. Immediate business being taken care of, the judge dismissed the group and Mrs. Dayton turned Craig over to Mr. Ark.

"Let's go home now, Craig," Mr. Ark said.

Chapter Seven

> *"The stately homes . . .*
> *How beautiful they stand,*
> *Amidst their tall ancestral trees*
> *O'er all the pleasant land!"*
> Felicia Hemans

On the way home from the county seat, Mr. Ark chatted nervously about all kinds of things, except what Craig expected—the tree. Craig responded with short grunts, but mostly kept quiet.

Mrs. Ark greeted Craig warmly, but thankfully she didn't try to hug him. "You all are just in time for lunch," she said. Craig knew she kept the books for Mr. Ark's carpet business and she worked a few days each week; today was not one of those. He guessed they had gotten most of the water damage cleaned up from the summer's powerful hurricane which flooded the store. Or maybe she stayed home to welcome him.

After lunch, Mrs. Ark took Craig upstairs. Siegfried bounded up the steps, leading the way.

"Let me help you with those crutches." Mrs. Ark reached for a crutch, causing Craig to stumble and drop it. "Maybe not." She picked it up and together they managed to prop it under Craig's arm.

"I think I can manage better by myself."

"The spare room is yours, Craig." Mrs. Ark led him down the hall and into the guest room. "You can share Nelson's bathroom. My husband is going back into work soon, and I'll be in the kitchen if you need anything." Mrs. Ark turned down the covers on the twin bed on the right. "I hope you will be comfortable here, Craig. Why don't you take a nap now?"

"I am kind of tired," Craig said.

Mrs. Ark left, but Siegfried stayed with Craig.

The view from the window of Craig's room looked down on the wild little butterfly garden that lay dormant, waiting for next spring's crop of butterflies.

When he heard the doorbell ring, Craig opened his bedroom door. "Keep quiet, Siegfried. Let's see who's here. It might be my dad." Confusion filled Craig's mind as he crept to the banister that circled the staircase on three sides. Careful not to reveal himself, Craig listened as Mrs. Ark opened the front door.

"Why, Marjorie. I hadn't expected to see you so soon. Do come in. Bentley is in the kitchen."

It was Mrs. Dayton, the social worker. Was she coming to check up on Craig already?

"Thank you, Lisa. Is Craig here?"

Craig heard the door close with a gentle click.

"Yes, he's napping at the moment. Do you want me to wake him?"

"That won't be necessary, I…"

"Hello, Marjorie," Craig heard Mr. Ark say. "I'm glad you're here. We have something important we want to discuss with you."

"Come on back to the kitchen, Marjorie," Mrs. Ark said, "and have some tea."

Mr. Ark spoke. "I hope this isn't going against the law, Marjorie, but what do you think about slowing down the search for Charlie? Lisa and I want Craig to stay with us for as long as it takes to reroute his life."

"That might be a few months, Bentley."

"We don't care. If you could manage to stall…?"

The voices faded out and Craig heard the kitchen door close.

Anyway, Craig didn't need to eavesdrop any further. If Mrs. Dayton could do what Mr. Ark requested, then she would be forestalling Craig's return home. Mr. Ark was such a sap. He couldn't even tell Craig was dying to get out on his own. *If it takes long enough to find Dad, I'll be well and outta here. I'll never have to live with that man again.* With that thought to comfort him, Craig fell into a much-needed nap beside Siegfried.

* * * *

A little after three o'clock, Craig heard the school bus stop in front of the house. Soon there was a knock on the guest room door.

"Yeah?" Craig responded.

"Can I come in, Craig?" Nelson called.

It's your house, Nelson. "Sure," Craig said, "come on

in."

Nelson opened the door and stood there. "Hi, Craig. How you feeling?"

"Hi," said Craig. "So-so."

"Hey, Sieg," said Nelson. Siegfried barked and waggled his body where he sat on the bed with Craig, but he didn't jump down to greet his master.

"I hope you're going to like living here, Craig." Nelson looked down at his feet, squirming. He stood with his hands behind his back, his neck hunched into his shoulders.

"What difference does it make?" Craig spoke tight-lipped. He hated feeling like an outsider. "I'm not here to like it. It's my punishment."

"That's not true. We asked you here because we didn't want you to get hurt anymore!"

Craig had never seen Nelson so angry before.

"Well, the judge said I have to take care of the tree."

"So? Why shouldn't you? The tree might die and you're the one to blame. Don't you have the guts to admit it?"

"You don't know everything, Nelson. Maybe I had my reasons."

"Reasons! Yeah?" Nelson said, bitterly, backing into the hall. "Whatever."

Craig turned his face away. There. He had done it again. Hurt someone before he even knew himself what he was going to say. But who was hurt worse? He probably wouldn't last here long. They'd kick him out—before he was even healed.

"Come on, Siegfried," Nelson said.

But Siegfried stayed on the bed with Craig.

* * * *

Later, Craig joined the Ark family for dinner. He sat quietly and picked at his food as the family talked their regular talk and gave him his space. Only Siegfried, lying with his head on Craig's foot, seemed really glad Craig was there.

At bedtime, Mrs. Ark came into Craig's room. "Here are your clothes I brought from your house this afternoon, Craig." She opened a drawer in the chest and arranged his folded clothes. "I couldn't find any pajamas, so you can borrow these of Mr. Ark's." Craig knew her little chuckle was supposed to make him feel at ease. "I think Nelson's pjs are too short for you. You can turn these up at the bottom." She reached out and brushed Craig's hair back from his forehead. Craig turned away fearing his eyes would fill up with tears, not because he didn't want Mrs. Ark to touch him, but because the touch reminded him of his mother.

Mrs. Ark moved to where Siegfried stretched out at the foot of the bed and patted him on the head, saying, "I see Siegfried has adopted you, Craig. You can be responsible for him now; feeding him will be one of your chores."

So they're not kicking me out—at least, not yet.

Mrs. Ark smiled and said, "Goodnight, you two."

Craig put on the pjs and climbed into bed. He was secretly pleased he was assigned to take care of their family pet. He'd always liked Siegfried. As he rested his hand on the dog's back and drowsed off to sleep, Craig knew he had one real friend in the world.

Chapter Eight

*"Get up, sweet Slug-a-bed, and see
The dew bespangling herb and tree."*
Robert Herrick

Craig woke refreshed on Saturday morning. He decided to bide his time about hitting the road again. He knew he wouldn't get far with his leg in this condition. Anyway, this was pretty cushy punishment.

Siegfried had spent much of Friday in Craig's room. Friday evening, Mr. Ark said they would see what could be done about the tree tomorrow.

Well, today was tomorrow, and Craig was ready to tackle the job.

After breakfast, when Mrs. Ark changed his bandage, Craig winced, but did not cry out. "The wound looks good; it isn't infected." She peered intently at his face and smiled. "And your eye doesn't look so bad today. The swelling has nearly gone from your lip, too."

Craig averted his eyes.

"We have regular Saturday chores to do," Mrs. Ark explained. "I'm off to the farmers' market." She was wearing a different sweat suit today. "Nelson will help his dad wash the truck and then the K'BeTs officers are coming over here."

She paused for a moment, replacing ointments in the First Aid Kit. "I want you to rest and make yourself at home. You may watch TV if you like."

"Thanks," Craig said. But after she left, he picked up his crutches and went out to the back porch. "Come on, Siegfried."

Stepping onto the back porch was like stepping into another dimension. Fog surrounded the house, shrinking Craig's world into this little acre and distancing him from all else. Closing the door behind the dog, Craig took a deep breath and forced himself to look at the tree. It stood as always in its corner of the lawn, shrouded in a veil of luminous mist.

Craig carefully descended the steps and moved into the fog. As he crossed the backyard, he looked for changes in the tree. It stood stalwart and green. It didn't look so very different except for the lighter colored band encircling the trunk. Chips and sawdust on the ground gave evidence of the assault.

Thinking back two days, Craig could hardly believe it was he who had done that terrible thing. *It couldn't have been me.* But, wait. Yes, it was. He remembered every nuance of feeling that flooded his mind and body that day. The fear. The jealousy turning to hatred. The rage.

That was me. But not the real me.

It was someone Craig wanted to forget, to leave behind. He wanted to run away from that person as much as he wanted to run away from his dad. And he would do it, too—when the right time came.

Nelson thought he was a coward; that he wouldn't live up to what he had done. "I'm not a coward!" Craig protested. The feeling he had been trying to bury now surfaced. He made himself confront his malicious behavior. He faced his guilt squarely. He remembered how he tried to cut down the tree. How heartless he had been. He was guilty and he regretted what he had done. The realization had a grip on his throat.

Craig looked up into the green foliage, and as he did, drops of condensed water on the leaves dropped onto his face. He wiped his hand across his eyes. Not all of the dampness was from the fog. Tears of remorse mingled with the mist. The long moment slowly spun itself out.

Now sunlight filtered through the branches of the tree. As the fog dissolved, the gnawing pain of guilt was overpowered by an even stronger emotion. Craig wanted to repair the tree. But how? What could he do? What should he be doing now?

A solution came to him. Fertilizer. Of course. He would spread fertilizer around the tree and that would heal its wound.

As quickly as he could, restrained by pain and the crutches, Craig returned to the utility shed where he found the chain saw two days before. Siegfried followed him.

A bag of fertilizer leaned against the wall and the spreader stood beside it. Craig tossed his crutches aside. He fumbled with the string holding the bag closed and ripped it off. He poured fertilizer into the spreader. Siegfried took a whiff, sneezed, and backed away. Using the spreader for support, Craig wheeled it out and over to the big oak. He pressed the release, and as he limped around the tree, the white fishy-smelling powder flowed out. *This ought to do it. I'll sprinkle water on the fertilizer and it will soak in overnight.*

Craig was startled when he heard Mr. Ark demand, "What do you think you're doing, Craig?"

"I'm fertilizing the tree," he said. "I'm doing what the judge said." His voice had an edge to it. "I'm mending the tree." *What was wrong with the man?*

"Oh, Craig!" said Mr. Ark. "Don't you understand? You cut through the growth layer. Fertilizer isn't going to do any good."

The pronouncement sliced into Craig's resolve. His good intentions lay around his feet like sawdust. He imagined the tree as it was before. He clung to a scrap of hope before it all evaporated. There had to be some way to repair the tree.

Craig squared his shoulders and faced Mr. Ark. He asked bitterly, "What's wrong with you? Last night you said you'd fix it! You've given up, haven't you?" But just because Mr. Ark had lost his determination was no reason for Craig to. "What can I do then?" He had a real stake in this now. "Is there someone I can call? Please, Mr. Ark."

Craig watched as Mr. Ark did some mental calculations. He knew Mr. Ark wanted to save the tree as much as he did. He leaned toward Mr. Ark, his whole body tight.

Mr. Ark ran his hand through his hair, mussing the neat comb-job. "There is someone who might be able to help.

Logan Raxter. I'll call and see if he'll come out. But don't get your hopes up."

Craig couldn't help but get his hopes up; far back in his throat he felt a little tickle of elation. The muscles of his face and shoulders relaxed as he went to the shed to retrieve his crutches, again leaning on the spreader for support. "Come on, Siegfried," he called, almost cheerily.

Mr. Ark preceded him into the house, but Craig had to pass through the gauntlet: Nelson and the three other K'BeTs officers were gathered on the back porch. The K'BeTs had seen the tree.

As Craig and Siegfried crossed the porch, no one spoke, but Carson had her hands on her hips as she glared at him. The look of scorn on their faces was more than Craig could take. His high spirits turned to defiance and he frowned.

"What are you looking at?" he mumbled and hurried into the house.

Mr. Ark's den was to the right of the back door. Craig found Mr. Ark there finishing a telephone conversation. "Thanks so much, Logan," he said, "we'll expect you soon, then." Replacing the receiver, he looked at Craig and rubbed his hands together. "Okay, Craig." He actually smiled. "The best forester I know is on his way here. Let's see if he can perform a miracle."

Craig followed Mr. Ark into the kitchen. "Would you like a glass of orange juice, Craig, while we wait for Logan?"

"Yes, please."

Mr. Ark poured coffee for himself and juice for Craig.

Seated at the kitchen table, they heard loud angry voices coming from the back porch. The meeting of the K'BeTs was not going well.

"I wonder what's gotten into the K'BeTs," Mr. Ark said. "They used to be so tight, always thinking about ways to create a 'better tomorrow.' But now it seems as if there has been a split."

"Yeah," Craig said. "I heard Nelson talking about it. They can't decide on their next service project."

"I'm ba-ack!" Mrs. Ark called from the garage. She returned from the farmers' market laden with fresh fruits and vegetables. Mr. Ark helped her carry in her bags through the laundry room. He didn't ask Craig to help, as he would have in the old days.

"My goodness," said Mrs. Ark, after all the food had been stowed in the refrigerator. "I have never heard the K'BeTs acting like this before." She looked out onto the porch. "I have a good mind to go out there and adjourn the meeting."

"I wouldn't do that," Mr. Ark said. "Let them work out their problems themselves." Then he said, "Lisa, Logan Raxter is on his way here to take a look at the tree."

Mrs. Ark paused in folding a paper bag. She looked at her husband and then at Craig. "That's fine," she said quietly, "you couldn't have chosen a better expert."

Mr. Ark and Craig finished waiting on the front porch. When a green truck turned into the driveway, Mr. Ark exclaimed, "There's Logan now." He hurried to greet him.

After shaking hands, the two men approached the tree, talking. Craig followed, slowed by his crutches. Siegfried greeted the visitor and ran back to escort Craig.

Mr. Logan Raxter walked around the tree, ducking under the six-foot branch. He shook his head.

It was with reluctance Craig joined the men, seeing it as one more hurdle he had to vault.

Mr. Ark introduced Craig and Mr. Raxter and then left them alone. Mr. Raxter did not shake Craig's hand, yet he said nothing about Craig's part in the tree's condition. A powerfully built man, dressed in lumberjack plaid, heavy boots, and baseball cap, Mr. Raxter gently extended his hands and placed them like a healer on the wound of the tree. That simple movement told Craig Mr. Raxter would use not just his knowledge, but also his will to restore health to this tree.

"Let me mull this over for a few minutes, Craig," Raxter said. "Why don't you go over there with those other kids till I call you back?"

"Those other kids" happened to be the K'BeTs on the back porch. Craig had no intention of joining them, so he wandered over to the rose garden and sat on the white iron bench. He tilted his face up to the sun; autumn weather sure was nice here in north Florida.

The harshness of the club discussion abated. Apparently, the members had worked their problems out for themselves, as Mr. Ark hoped they would. The tone of the meeting now sounded congenial.

"That's a great idea you have there, Nelson," Carson

said.

"You convinced me," Jean said.

"Yeah," Shaquan said. "I wish I thought of it myself. We can build a skateboard ramp for our next service project."

"Hey," Carson said, "aren't you getting ahead of yourself, Shaquan?"

"Now, we're through arguing," Jean said. "We've all agreed the tree should be our service project. Let's go talk it over with Mr. Raxter."

The K'BeTs rushed down the steps and sprinted over to talk to the tree man. "Hi, Mr. Raxter," they each said.

"Hello, there, K'BeTs."

"Mr. Raxter, we want to ask you something," Shaquan said. "Can we help you with the tree?"

"What he means is," Carson said, "we want the tree to be our service project."

"That is," Jean said, "if there is anything we can do."

"I'm sure we can find something for you to do. You were a big help to me after Hurricane Daisy."

Craig was astounded. That bunch had a lot of nerve. The tree was his project. Who invited them? He hobbled over to the tree.

Mr. Raxter seemed pleased with the offer of help from the club. "We're going to have extra help, Craig," he said. "And believe me we're going to need it." He didn't even give Craig a say in the matter. The prospect of working with that bunch of do-gooders put Craig in a glum mood for the rest of the day.

After walking around the tree several times, Mr. Raxter said, "I'll let you guys know what to do as soon as I figure it out myself. Right now, I need to go to town to get some supplies."

Mrs. Ark called the young people into the kitchen for lunch. Afterward, she insisted Craig get some rest before any more activity. Craig whistled for Siegfried, and as the two headed for the stairs, Craig heard Carson say, "I can't see why Siegfried wants to hang around that Craig."

Chapter Nine

"The best friend of man on earth is the tree."
Frank Lloyd Wright

Mrs. Ark excused Craig from church on Sunday morning. "Just this once," she said.

Later, after a hasty lunch, everyone jumped into work clothes.

Craig was in the kitchen with the Arks when Raxter bounded up the back steps and knocked on the door. "We're ready to get started, if you folks are," he said. The family, Craig, and Siegfried followed him. Raxter had not come alone.

Motioning to a group of men who were milling around the side yard, he said, "I think you know most of the fellows. These men all work for the utility company. They've volunteered to help us out today. Word about the tree has spread all over town, and lots of people have offered to help any way they can."

Mr. Ark shook hands all round with the utility crew. They in turn murmured hellos and condolences for the tree's condition. Craig noticed how some of the men looked askance at him, but no one said anything directly to him.

Craig looked out to the road and saw a big utility truck, its bucket lever folded back like a bent elbow. When extended, the "arm" would lift the bucket fifty feet into the air. "Is that a cherry picker?" asked Nelson.

"Sure is, son," answered one of the utility crewmen.

"What is that for?" Mrs. Ark asked.

"Well," Raxter said, "I'm sorry, Lisa, but we're going to have to take drastic measures. We need to prune some branches off the tree. The utility truck is our best means of getting to the top branches."

"Well, that's fine, if you think you must," Mr. Ark said, "but how do you plan to bring the truck up to the tree?"

"That's where things get sticky," said Raxter. "If we come up the driveway we'll have to plow through the rose garden. Or we could cut down some of the camellias lining the road and come at the tree by the edge of the woods."

"Oh, my goodness," squealed Mrs. Ark. "You surely wouldn't go through my prize roses."

"Well, it's up to you, Lisa." Raxter tilted his head.

Craig hated to see the pained expression on Mrs. Ark's face. But he admired her when she straightened her back, put her lips together in determination, and gave a single nod of her head. "Take out as many of the camellias as you need to," she said. "But, please try not to trample the roses."

Soon the volunteers were at work cutting down the camellias to make a path to the tree. Before the work was done, the K'BeTs arrived, all sixteen of them. Their sponsor, Mrs. Day—Jean's mom, and some other parents accompanied them. The youngsters gathered around Nelson rather than Craig, who was hanging back. The parents watched the utility crew, some offering to help. Raxter directed the removal of the camellia litter, and it did not take long with so many helping hands. There were only tight green buds on the bushes since they were not due to bloom until December.

"Out of the way, now, everybody," yelled Raxter, as the big truck lurched through the ditch beside the road and up the other side onto the Ark property. By now, both sides of the road were crowded with the parked cars of townspeople who had come to offer assistance or to gawk. One lady was dressed for a party, but that didn't stop her. Some of the work was done by a group of monks from Tibet. During the course of the day, hundreds of people slowly drove by or stopped to see what was going on.

The driver of the truck made his way to the tree, skirting the rose garden. One of the utility workers climbed into the bucket and was hoisted to the highest extension. For several hours, Raxter directed the utility crew as they took turns cutting out the branches he had chosen for pruning. It was noisy, dirty, backbreaking work. When the job was finished, the crowd was aghast.

Craig overheard the dressed-up lady say, "The tree is no longer the beautiful, symmetrical, specimen of fame."

Silently, Craig agreed. *Reminds me of a movie star whose toupee has been snatched off. The tree has lost its dignity.*

But Raxter was not a man easily put off. "At least," he said, "this will take some of the stress off the tree. If it lives, we can shape it up better, later."

Looking at Mr. Ark, Craig saw the taut muscles of the man's face as he fought tears of dismay.

"Okay," yelled Raxter, "let's get the cherry picker out of the way so the tree can get a long, tall drink."

He had contacted not only the utility crew but the local volunteer firemen, as well. It was now time for the firemen to take their turn. The fire truck, which carried seven hundred and fifty gallons of water, replaced the utility truck. Several men held on to the nozzle of the hose and sprayed a stream of water into the air. Water came down on the tree like rain.

Nor was Raxter yet done engaging the help of the community. Another truck pulled onto the property. A big fancy hotel down near the beach sent over a load of leaf mulch. The truck backed onto the lawn and dumped the mulch close to the tree. Craig stayed out of sight when Raxter and the Arks thanked the driver and all the other volunteers.

Shadows of dusk darkened the sky. All of the friends, the K'BeTs, and the volunteers, left. Only Raxter remained. The Arks and Craig gathered around him, thanking him for his great effort and for organizing all the help.

"Hey," he said, "this is just the beginning. For starters, tomorrow, I want Craig to spread the mulch around the tree."

Nelson spoke up. "Mr. Raxter, the K'BeTs want to help too, remember. The tree's our service project."

"Thanks, Nelson." Raxter clapped the boy on the shoulder. "With that injury of his, Craig will need the help."

"I'm getting rid of these crutches tomorrow," Craig said. "I've had it with these things."

Mrs. Ark tweaked his ear. "We'll see what the doctor has to say about that."

Chapter Ten

"These trees shall be my books."
Shakespeare - AS YOU LIKE IT

Monday dawned clear and cool. It would have been a good day to play football, if Craig weren't injured and if there were anyone who would play with him. But football was out of the question, and Craig was an outcast among the students.

The previous evening, as the weary family finished the busy day, Craig had approached Mrs. Ark expectantly. "May I stay home from school tomorrow, Mrs. Ark? Just one day—really. Mr. Raxter is starting some kind of special treatment for the tree." Craig wanted to be there. He needed to be there.

"I have to take you to see Dr. Leopold, anyway," she said, granting him permission.

The checkup went well, and the doctor said Craig might put the crutches away for at least part of the time.

"Craig," Mrs. Ark said, after they came home from the clinic, "I want you to wear my husband's old jacket to work in." She didn't mention there was no jacket among his belongings she brought from his house on Friday.

"It's too big for me." In truth, Craig was embarrassed.

"It's only for today. We're going to have to get you some new things. The weather has turned quite chilly."

"But I don't want to go shopping," Craig said.

"I'll take care of it," she said. "I'll go later today."

Raxter arrived and backed his truck into the yard close to the tree.

Craig joined him in the backyard, minus the crutches and wearing Mr. Ark's jacket.

"What have you got there?" Craig asked.

"I've got a bunch of live oak cuttings. You've probably heard of grafting, haven't you?"

"Yeah, I think so."

"That's what we're going to do here. We're going to graft the young sprouts to the old tree. We're going to bridge the gap over the cut and reroute the sap." Raxter made bridging motions with his hand. "This is called bridge grafting."

"How many will it take?"

"I figure we'll need over a hundred." Raxter lifted a picnic cooler out of the back of the truck. "I have some here I took from the woods behind my house, but we're going to need more."

"Should I bring over this other cooler?"

"No, wait till we finish this bunch. But you can bring over that can of grafting wax."

Craig found the can of wax and took it to Raxter.

"What's this for?"

"This will help anchor the scions in place and prevent germs from getting inside."

"Scions?" Craig said. He had only seen the lofty word in books about kings and princes.

"It means a child, a descendant," Raxter said. "In this case, a young tree."

"In books, they talk about the prince being the 'scion.'" said Craig.

"So, you're a reader, are you?" asked Raxter, smiling.

"Some," said Craig. "I mostly like sports books. And some knights and stuff."

"I like sports books, too." Raxter lifted his chin and put on a mock-uppity expression. "But, I also like biography and books that use words like 'scion.' Now let's get to work."

Raxter's friendly tone eased Craig's tension.

"We'll go into the woods, here, Craig," Raxter said. "I want you to practice the grafting on a tree in the forest before you attempt any on the oak. There's an art to this."

Raxter showed Craig how to implant the little cuttings into a tree. "We'll have to straddle the cut. One end of the scion will go in above the cut and one below and be stuck in place with the wax. There's also some science to this. See here. The living tissue is in layers. Under the bark is the phloem layer which conducts the sap. Next to that is the cambium layer. That's where growth takes place, and it's only one cell thick. If we're successful, the water and sap can run up and down as if nothing happened."

"I sure hope it works," said Craig.

Raxter nodded his head and set to work. He melted the wax as it was needed over a can of Sterno.

Craig was clumsy at first then quickly became proficient enough to begin on the oak. It was tiring work, bending over with arms outstretched all day, since the cut was at Craig's waist level.

"You're learning, Craig," said Raxter.

"Do you really think these little pieces can feed this big tree?" Craig asked.

"It does seem like a tall order." Raxter wiped sweat from his forehead. In spite of the cool air, the work was making them warm, so they both threw aside their jackets. "I've never treated a tree cut all the way around before. But I've had success with all kinds of grafting. All we can do is our best."

The two were silent for a while.

Before going shopping, Mrs. Ark brought the workers a Thermos of hot tea and a kneepad for Craig for when he did his work kneeling. Cautioning Craig not to overstress his leg, she said, "I'm going to get you a nice warm jacket. This cool spell has taken us by surprise."

"I don't like it, myself," said Raxter. "It worries me about the tree."

"Oh, I hadn't thought of that." Mrs. Ark's tone showed her concern. "Too bad we can't wrap it up in a blanket."

"Another thing that worries me is how to water the tree. We can't keep asking the fire department to come out here. Bentley told me your well is barely enough for your needs. I think we're going to have to dig another one."

"Well, you take it up with Bentley," said Mrs. Ark. "I'm going to run to town now. And Craig," she said, as she went to the garage, "your lunch is in the refrigerator. I'm leaving Siegfried with you."

"Craig," said Raxter, "I think you have the hang of this. You continue with the grafting. I'm going into the woods to get some more cuttings from oak trees."

Left alone, Craig worked until lunchtime then shared with Siegfried the lunch Mrs. Ark left for him. She also left strict instructions for him to rest for at least half an hour after lunch, so Craig watched TV for a while. There was really nothing interesting on—some stupid soap operas, kiddie cartoons, how to decorate your house, stuff like that, and besides, his leg wasn't hurting much, so he went back outside.

Raxter had returned and begun grafting the new pieces onto the tree. "I don't want to cut too many at a time; I want them to be as fresh as possible when they're attached," he explained. He continued to make trips into the woods during the afternoon.

Craig worked steadily until he heard the school bus stop at the end of the front walk. Nelson got off accompanied by a group of the K'BeTs. Craig had forgotten they wanted to help with the tree. By now, Mrs. Ark was home. She served the kids an after-school snack on the back porch and called Craig to join them, but he declined. He didn't blame her; he knew she was clueless.

Craig muttered under his breath. "The K'BeTs don't want me any more than I want them."

When the group came over to the tree, Shaquan said, "What are you doing, Craig?"

"I'm putting in some bridge grafts," Craig said.

"Oh, listen to Mr. Smarty-pants," said Carson. "He sounds like he really knows what he's doing."

"Be quiet, Carson," whispered Jean. "Do you want us to help you, Craig?"

"No," he said. "I think you better not unless Mr. Raxter says it's all right. But you could start spreading mulch." He pointed to the big pile of leaf mulch that the hotel had sent over and dumped near the tree.

"Okay," Nelson said. "Let's go to the shed and get some shovels and things."

Nelson and the others brought tools from the shed and set to work. They horsed around almost as much as they worked, but much of the job was done by the time Raxter returned with more scions.

"Hi, guys," he called.

"Hey, Mr. Raxter," they all returned his greeting.

When he saw what the gang had done, he said, "You're doing a great job with the mulch, kids, if the state of your clothes and faces is an indication." Examining Craig's work, he said, "And your grafting is getting better, Craig."

"Thanks." How Craig needed Raxter's approval.

Before long, parents came to pick up the K'BeTs, and Mrs. Ark called Nelson and Craig in to dinner. Nelson said goodnight to Raxter and went into the house.

Craig lingered. "Will we finish the grafting tomorrow, Mr. Raxter? There's several feet of trunk still left to fix."

"No, Craig, I need to finish this tonight."

"I'll stay and help you."

"You go on in, Craig. You'll be going to school tomorrow. Right now, I have to go into town and make arrangements for some light."

With reluctance, Craig went in to dinner.

Long after the others were asleep, Craig looked out an upstairs window and saw Raxter working on the grafts by a glow of soft light. The portable lighting fixtures which provided the light were trailing cords leading to a volunteer fire department truck. The generator in the truck was crooning a midnight healing song. Craig marveled at how people in town were so willing and eager to help the tree recapture its vitality.

Quietly, Craig slipped out of the house to answer the lure of the tree. He helped Raxter until the hundred and thirty-eighth scion was firmly in place.

* * * *

The next morning, Craig limped to the bus stop and accompanied Nelson to school; there was no getting out of it. Mrs. Ark, with Siegfried, walked to the road with the boys, as if she wanted to protect Craig from the harsh words and ugly glances she knew would be coming his way that day. He knew it wouldn't make an impression on these hostile judges.

And how right he was. The usual early morning chatter on the bus quieted as he and Nelson took their seats. But as soon as the bus pulled away from Mrs. Ark, the goading began.

"Hoot! Hoot! Hoot!"

"What got into you, buzz boy?"

"Why don't you pick on something your own size?"

Craig sat stone-faced looking out the window. Only once did he steal a glance at Carson, who did not join in the taunting, but rather seemed sorrowful.

The worst was when one of the older boys said, "Did you hear the one about the guy who looked up his family tree and found out that he was the sap?" Howls of laughter erupted from several of the more rowdy clowns.

"Hey, Craig. Why don't you make like a tree—and leaf?"

The ridicule only stopped when Nelson yelled, "Hey, cut it out, you guys."

They didn't know Craig was sorry for what he had done, and there was no way he was going to tell them. So he passed the day without talking to anyone, going to class alone, eating lunch alone, his face frozen into a sullen mask. The only person who was nice to him was Nelson, who met up with him at the school bus to go home. He was glad the day was over.

Chapter Eleven

*"I am the Lorax.
I speak for the trees."*
Dr. Seuss

After Craig and Nelson changed into work clothes and had their snack, they went out to the tree. Logan Raxter was there.

"Have you been here all day, Mr. Raxter?" Nelson asked.

"No, Nelson. I just got here. But I came in this morning to sprinkle water on the grafts I did in the dark last night."

Nelson laughed. "I've heard of people knowing things so well they could do them in their sleep."

"Mr. Raxter's kidding," Craig said. "He was out here at midnight, but he had some light."

"Yes, thanks to our friends at the fire department. And I had some help as well." He smiled at Craig.

"Here come some of the K'BeTs." Nelson waved them over.

When the group joined them, Raxter said, "The only thing for you to do today is climb up the tree and take off as much of the Spanish moss as you can. Stuff it into these bags."

"That's neat," said Gary. "I've always loved to play in

this tree."

"Me, too," said Norma Faith. "Somebody give me a boost."

"Now wear these gloves," said Raxter. "I don't want any of you to get bit by chiggers."

The K'BeTs tackled the task of gathering Spanish moss with pleasure.

"Is that all we're going to do for the tree?" Craig felt as if more should be done.

"No, there's plenty more for us to do, but we need supplies first."

"What kind of supplies?" Shaquan asked.

"The tree needs high pH water; we're going to drill a deep well so the tree will have all the water it needs."

"Who's going to pay for it?" Carson—always the practical one.

"Well, umm." Raxter mulled. "I'm going to talk to Mr. Ark about that when he returns from his trip. And there might be other things we'll need, also."

"Wow," said Shaquan. "This is getting expensive. Have we got any money in the K'BeTs treasury, Jean?"

"A little," Jean said. "Do you all want me to give it to Mr. Raxter?"

"Yeah," the rest of the K'BeTs responded, except Nelson.

"We're missing a few members," he said. "This is something the whole club should decide on."

"You're right," Jean said. "Nelson, you should call a

special meeting."

"Or you could call them on the phone." Again—Carson the efficient one.

"Yeah, I'll do that," said Nelson. He ran into the house to make the calls.

Motorists passing by slowed down or stopped to take a closer look at the tree just as they had done all weekend. People continued to try to get a close look at what was going on at the Ark home. Craig hated to be stared at, so he turned away. The K'BeTs also noticed the observers.

"I'll bet those people would like to pitch in and help the tree." [BB1]Carson was not the timid type. "Let's ask them for some money."

The K'BeTs and Craig and Raxter stopped what they were doing. *Well, why not?* they all seemed to be thinking.

"Why don't we put up a donation box?" said Jean. She was more reserved than Carson. "Then people can be as generous as they can."

"I like that idea, too," said Raxter. "I'll make a box now."

The K'BeTs went into the house to tell Nelson and ask how the phone calls were going, and Craig helped Raxter build the donation box.

* * * *

When Mr. Ark returned from an out-of-town trip, the box was in place near the Ark mailbox. Raxter lost no time in getting the new well drilled as soon as Mr. Ark said he would fund it.

Craig watched the K'BeTs working hard for the tree. They wanted to collect as much money as possible, so they contacted the newspapers, the radio stations, and the TV station in the city. *It's working like a charm,* Craig thought. Generous people from every surrounding town came by.

* * * *

"The donation box is a success," Raxter said to Craig one day. The two of them were inspecting the grafts.

"I know. Mrs. Ark has been emptying it at least once a day."

"When people feel close to something, they will give with open hand. And somehow, this tree has brought people together—has opened people's hearts. It's like the tree sent out invisible waves, or like a fisherman throwing out a net and hauling in a great catch of love." Raxter's voice quavered as he made his impassioned speech; he seemed to have surprised himself. "It's funny how so many things get connected. I guess everything is connected to everything else in this old world. Did you ever hear about the Sierra Club?"

"Yeah, Nelson belongs."

"The man who started it, John Muir, said, 'Whenever we try to isolate anything in the universe we find that it's hitched up to everything else.'"

Raxter's speech made Craig uncomfortable. It hit too close to his bruised heart. His mother was gone for good and his dad was now out of his life. "Well, I'm not hitched to anything!" he said.

The expression of thoughtful camaraderie on Raxter's

face abruptly changed to one of unbelieving pain. He opened his mouth to say something; Craig thought he was going to contradict him. But Raxter said nothing—just stood there looking as if he had been slapped. Then Craig walked off, limping into the woods, Siegfried following.

Other donations came to Mr. Ark's home address by mail. Mrs. Ark put a guest book in the donation box for visitors to sign. Some of the donors were from places as far away as Australia or as close as the nearby Biophilia Nature Center. Many of the people who stopped got out of their cars and offered to help with the manual labor. Everyone was elated. Everyone, that is, except Craig.

Craig did not like to believe his actions caused this massive upheaval. His offence was the focus of widespread sympathy, and ironically, goodwill. Every time a stranger stopped, Craig wanted to sink into the ground; he wished he could disappear. If he stood still, he was taken to be one of the K'BeTs. But if he moved, his limp gave him away as the boy who wounded the tree. Raxter never let anyone say anything to Craig. Craig just went about his business with downcast eyes so he could not see the puzzlement, anger and disgust in the eyes of strangers.

Within a week of making the arrangements for a four-inch diameter well, the one-hundred-and forty-foot deep well had been drilled. Raxter scrounged a sixty-five-foot power pole onto which he attached a two-inch PVC pipe line so the well water could be sprayed onto the tree from the top. The well, the two-hundred-gallon water tank, and the one horsepower pump cost nearly three thousand dollars.

The weather continued to get cooler. Halloween came and went without much fanfare at the Ark household. Mrs. Dayton checked on Craig every week.

One afternoon, Raxter said to Craig, "You know—I've been thinking about what Mrs. Ark said about wrapping the tree up in a blanket. Well, she said too bad we couldn't. But I'm thinking we can. We're going to put a tent around the tree."

"I don't see how." Craig was disbelieving. "It would take a circus tent to cover the tree."

"We don't need a tent to cover the whole tree. We'll build one to go around the lower trunk. They're predicting this winter will be a cold one."

"I'm pretty sure it is. You know that jacket Mrs. Ark bought me? It's been feeling real good on these cold mornings."

Raxter nodded and twisted his mouth into a sucking sound. "So we're going to have to buy a heater."

At dinner, Mr. Ark brought up another disturbing fact. Although some gifts were still dribbling in, most of the donated funds had been spent.

That night when Craig and Nelson were studying together at the kitchen table, Craig told Nelson Raxter wanted to buy a tent and a heater for the tree.

Craig said, "I wish I had the money to buy a heater."

"Dad hasn't got the money either," Nelson said. He sat with his chin cupped in his hand. After thinking about the situation for a minute, Nelson's head jerked up. "I've got an idea. We could have a fundraiser. The K'BeTs can do it."

Chapter Twelve

> *"It may be that some little root of the sacred tree still lives. Nourish it then, that it may leaf and bloom and fill with singing birds."*
> Black Elk
> Oglala Sioux Chief

The next day at school, Nelson called a mini-meeting during lunch and the K'BeTs enthusiastically embraced the idea of a fundraiser. And that evening, Jean called to say her mother had given permission.

"That's great!" Nelson punched the air. "Now we can brainstorm to decide what to do."

"I'll help, too," Mrs. Ark said. But Mr. Ark did not say anything. He seemed to be in a mood as dark as the cup of coffee he was staring into. He wasn't even fidgeting.

"What's wrong, Bentley?" Mrs. Ark asked. "Don't you like the idea of a fundraiser? Every little bit will help."

"We're going to need a lot more than a little bit," Mr. Ark said. He got up from the table and went into the den, leaving the door open. The people in the kitchen heard him make a telephone call. When he returned, he said, "I just talked to David Larsen. I'm going into the bank tomorrow to apply for a loan."

"Gosh," Nelson said. He seemed as surprised at this news as Craig was. Craig thought, *I could leave now, but it wouldn't make any difference. Mr. Ark would still pour every cent he has into the tree.* He went to bed depressed.

* * * *

After school the next day, Craig and Nelson joined Raxter and Mr. Torrey Bartram, the owner of a hardware store, in erecting a shelter around the tree. Each of the four sides was framed to be twenty feet long by ten feet high. Plastic windows across the top allowed light to stream in for the scions, and a door permitted entrance. The boys helped the men nail yards and yards of clear plastic sheeting to the top of the frame and bring it together in a bunch around the trunk and lower limbs of the tree. Craig was happy to have something strenuous to do. He nailed planks in place with the force of a John Henry.

To Craig, the tree continued to look normal. Sure, it was dropping some leaves, that was to be expected in late autumn. There were still lots of green leaves on the live oak. Maybe the tree was conserving her strength to forge through the winter. Did she feel connected to the people who were working so hard to save her? Did she remember being at the center of a large community? Did she miss the squirrels scampering in her canopy? The birds raising nests-full of young? Would she be disappointed in the spring if there were no dragonflies or love bugs sheltering in her shade? Would she be sad if she had no shade to give? *At least the woodpeckers are not driven off by the noise and activity,* thought Craig; *they're still digging for insects standing upright against the trunk in that funny way they have.*

While Craig finished pounding on the last boards, Mr. Bartram helped Raxter lift an old water trough from the back of the truck. "Where did you scrounge this thing up, Logan?"

"I prefer to call it a 'donated item.'" Raxter laughed. "It came from the McCormick Farm." They dragged the plastic-lined trough into the shelter. "Craig," said Raxter, "I want you to keep this trough filled with water. With the heat pump and five water bed heaters, it's going to stay hot in here. Talk about Florida humidity—this will be extreme."

Nelson started painting the outside of the shelter. Mr. Bartram had[BB2] brought over several gallons of white paint. Craig joined Nelson.

"This reminds me of a hospital," said Craig, who had spent more time than he liked to think of in emergency rooms.

"We're giving the tree intensive care," said Nelson. "They call it 'ICU' for short."

"We could paint ICU on the sides here," said Craig.

"Yeah, let's do it," said Nelson. "I'll see if Dad has any red paint." He brought paint and brushes, and the two boys painted the letters on the sides of the shelter along with red crosses. When they were done, Nelson held up his hand and Craig responded with a high-five. His heart swelled; that was the first good feeling he'd had in a long time.

But Mr. Ark was acting peculiarly. He always seemed distracted. Sometimes he called from town to say he was working late, and Craig and Nelson would not see him the entire evening. The day after he made the phone call to Mr. Larsen, he explained how he had gone to the bank and took out a loan. He surprised everyone by coming home driving an old VW bug that had seen better days.

The family went into the garage to see the new car. "Don't feel bad, Bentley," said his wife, "the money from your nice truck will help pay for the tree's care." She patted his arm as she went back into the house.

"It's not so bad, Dad." Nelson wore the expression of one who has swallowed lemon juice.

Craig tried to cheer up Mr. Ark. Rubbing at a scratch mark on the VW, he said, "The K'BeTs are planning a fundraiser, you know."

"Yes, I know, Craig. Don't think I'm not grateful. It will help some, but it might not bring in enough money."

Mr. Ark passed a hand through his hair. "I've asked my wife to cancel our subscription to the newspaper and to cable TV."

Another of Mr. Ark's shockers.

"And no cell phones or new video games."

Bummer, thought Craig, but he didn't say it aloud. Better not draw attention to himself over something trivial like video games.

* * * *

The day after the ICU was completed, the heater arrived. The utility crew laid a special electrical hookup from the road and one of the electricians installed the heat pump. Everyone crowded into the greenhouse to watch Raxter throw the switch—Craig and Siegfried, Mr. and Mrs. Ark, Nelson and Carson. Lately, Carson often came home from school with the boys.

"That heater's humming like a '57 Thunderbird crusin' down the highway," said Mr. Ark. Everyone laughed.

"Now we'll see if we can make the tree believe it's spring," said Raxter.

After Raxter left, Mrs. Ark called everyone to dinner, inviting Carson along. Craig stayed behind. "I'll turn out the light," he said. He wanted to be alone with the tree. It was hard to say what he was feeling, because there were so many thoughts jumbled up in his head. Everyone had big hopes for the tree to survive the trauma. But why were they in this position? Why was everyone forced to work so hard? *It's because of me.* Craig's body tensed. *Oh, I wish I could go back and undo all the damage.* He walked to the tree and put his hands on it the way he had seen Raxter do that first day. He let out a long, loud sigh.

When he turned to go in to dinner, he saw Carson standing in the doorway of the ICU. Her animosity toward him had blown away, and now her eyes held a softness he had not seen before. They exchanged a brief but understanding look before Craig reached up and pulled the chain on the hanging light bulb. Then they walked silently into the house.

Chapter Thirteen

> *"Friendship is a sheltering tree."*
> Samuel Taylor Coleridge

The next Saturday, K'BeTs gathered in the Ark kitchen to brainstorm about their fundraiser. The officers acted as team leaders and formed groups with three other club members and started pitching out ideas. Each team hoped to come up with the best proposal.

Craig was sitting in front of the TV in the living room. He couldn't concentrate for straining to hear the voices in the kitchen. Siegfried stationed himself beside Craig.

Craig felt left out and it hurt. That was his tree. He sat fuming. When Mrs. Ark came into the living room with a feather duster, she said, in a fake French accent, "Mees-sure, do you mind eff I dust zeez *objects d'art?*"

He could tell she wanted to distract him. He made an attempt to accept her friendship. "Go right ahead, Ma-dame."

The *"objects d'art"* in question were the Noah's arks. Craig admired each item of the colorful and varied collection. *I wish my mom had had something pretty.* He could think about his mom a little now without much pain. Her curly brown hair that she had a hard time controlling in the Florida humidity. Her big green eyes. Sometimes Julia pushed Charlie into this job or that scheme, but he never held a job for long.

Craig remembered how his dad liked to go out with "the boys" and carouse a little and to drink a little. The drinking made it even harder to get a good job.

Finally, Julia persuaded Charlie to try his hand at roofing, a job he had irregular experience with. The bank wouldn't give him a loan, but Bentley Ark did. It went well for a while. Charlie stayed sober. They were about to make it. There was no health insurance because Julia was saving money to buy… Craig's thoughts were treading into a forbidden area. This was more painful than thoughts about the tree. He forced himself to smile at Mrs. Ark and make pleasant comments about her collection.

Before Craig had time to delve into self-pity again, Carson brought her group into the living room. "The teams are scattering because it got too noisy in the kitchen," she said. "Is it all right if we come in here?"

"Why, certainly," Mrs. Ark said, and left with her duster.

Craig clicked off the television and got up to leave with Siegfried following.

"Why don't you stay and help us, Craig?" Carson said. "We could use some more brain power." She looked at Mark and Norma Faith and Chan as if to dare them to dispute her.

They didn't. They nodded and mumbled, "Yeah, stay, Craig."

He hesitated then decided to stay. He wanted to be a part of the group and Carson was reaching out a hand in friendship. "Okay," he said. Since Craig returned to his seat,

Siegfried returned also, with his front half sitting beside Craig and his back half standing up.

"You're ridiculous, Siegfried," Chan said. Everyone laughed and the atmosphere in the room seemed friendly.

"Whatever we come up with," said Carson, slipping smoothly into the role of team leader, "had better be big. We can ask other people for help. I know for certain my mother's business will pitch in."

"My dad's Sunday school class will help, I bet," said Mark. Mark was a muscular boy with a shock of red hair who was never without a basketball. He twirled one on his finger during the meeting.

Norma Faith was the first with a suggestion. Twisting her hair around a scrunchy, she said, "Okay. I was thinking about a dog show. We take our poodle to dog shows, and it's expensive to enter. We could charge a lot. Everybody has a dog."

"Not everybody," said Chan. "But lots of people have pets. It doesn't have to be just dogs. James has rabbits and Nelson has Siegfried. I have a guinea pig. Her name is Tundra."

"A pet show is not big enough," said Carson. "But, it's a good suggestion," she added, when Norma Faith's face turned red. "I'll write that down. It's a good start."

"The weather's too cold for a dog wash or a car wash," said Mark. "They're always fun."

Craig cleared his throat, "Huh." He was going to jump in. "How about a bake sale?" he ventured. He had seen bake sales in front of the Food Lion.

Carson smiled at him across the coffee table and across the gulf of exclusion. Then she gently nixed his idea. "The Girl Scouts are selling cookies and the School Patrols are selling candy for their trip to Washington. I don't think a bake sale would go over right now. We need something totally different."

"I know," said Mark. "How about a chili cook-off?"

"Just chili?" asked Carson, wrinkling her nose.

"I wish we could do them all," whined Norma Faith, and pulled the scrunchy out of her hair.

Craig thought the way Carson tilted her head was cute. Then she surprised him by shouting, "Well, why don't we?"

She raised her arms into the air as if to embrace all the good ideas. "We could have a carnival in the school gym."

"And we could include whatever the other teams have come up with, too," Mark said.

"Let's go and see what they think about it." Carson jumped up and led the way to the kitchen. "I think it should be a winter carnival. We can rent a snow machine and everything."

Craig lagged back. It was nice while it lasted, but he didn't think the rest of the group would want him to butt in. And besides, Craig was expecting Mrs. Dayton. Every week, she advised him to be patient; his life would return to normal, eventually. At the time he had not believed her. But after today—with Carson—maybe she was right.

Mrs. Dayton arrived soon, and Craig told her about the

club meeting. It felt like a private thing, stock in his nearly depleted account of human dignity, but he was afraid not to tell her. He knew if the arrangement with the Arks did not work out, Mrs. Dayton would place him with a new family. That prospect called up the horrible vision of the forlorn trio from the shelter.

Raxter came to spray fertilizer on the grafts and the K'BeTs told him about their super idea—the entire group had agreed that a carnival *was* a super idea. And Raxter agreed it was the best way they could help the tree.

After the K'BeTs returned to the house, Craig joined Raxter. "What do you think about the tree?" he asked. "A lot of the scions have died."

Raxter let out a heavy sigh. "You're right, most of them, in fact. We're going to have to try a new tactic, something besides bridge grafting. Come here—let me show you." Raxter led the way to the back of his truck. "These babies are going to do the trick."

"Babies?" Craig thought Raxter was using slang.

"I do mean babies," said Raxter, pointing to the truck's cargo of potted plants. "We're going to plant these saplings in the ground around the tree and graft them above the cut. If we're lucky, the babies will feed the mother."

"How many did you bring?"

"I brought thirty-two. We'd better get started." He opened the back of the truck and lifted out two of the three-gallon pots.

"At least," said Craig, hefting one of the pots and

heading toward the shelter, "it's warmer in the ICU than it is out here. We step from fall into spring just by walking through this door."

Raxter laughed. "It's good to hear you lightening up." After a pause, he said, "Hey, Craig, do you know how the elephant got into the top of the oak tree?"

"No," said Craig, responding to Raxter's playful tone. "How did the elephant get into the top of the oak tree?"

"He sat on an acorn and waited," said Raxter. They both laughed heartily.

Grafting the young trees took the rest of the day. In some places the ground had to be built up with soil so the top of the little tree could reach above the cut on the large tree. Craig and Raxter now talked with ease, no tension between them.

"Mr. Raxter," Craig said, "why have you taken so many pains with this tree? I know it's the biggest and probably the oldest tree around, but there are others almost as big; and it's not an endangered species."

"It's a living thing, Craig. Every living thing has a right to its life. Sure—it's just one tree. Even so, I have respect for its very existence. There's potential in even one life that we can't imagine." He wiped sweat from his head with his forearm; it was warm and humid in the ICU. "I want to get it right this time. This may be our last chance to save the tree."

"I guess we'll have to be patient, like the elephant," said Craig.

Chapter Fourteen

"A culture is no better than its woods."
W. H. Auden

Craig hovered on the fringes of the group as they made their preparations. His facial wounds were healed and his limp was slight, so now he felt less conspicuous as the agent of the tree's wound. He went on some scrounging expeditions with Nelson and helped with posters and signs, but no one asked him to participate in the carnival itself. Not that he wanted to.

He liked being with Carson, now they were friends; she knew without his telling her how he felt—especially about the tree. One day, she, Nelson and Craig sat around the kitchen table making posters. Mrs. Ark provided supplies and encouragement.

"I heard your announcement for the carnival on the radio, Carson," Mrs. Ark said. "You've done an excellent job with the publicity."

Carson beamed. She tossed her wavy brown hair back from her face with a graceful flip. "It's been lots of fun; I've loved doing it. Ours is going to be the most authentic winter carnival in the 'Sunshine State.'"

* * * *

Craig was glad when the big day arrived because all he'd heard from the K'BeTs for weeks was "carnival, carnival, carnival." Let them have their fun. He would stay home and mope. Mr. Ark would soon be out of debt and the tree would grow strong.

The big day dawned cold and clear. Craig helped load Mrs. Ark's car with supplies for last minute touches. With his breath puffing white clouds of steam, he lifted Siegfried into the car and returned to the kitchen, shivering.

Mrs. Ark peeked around the door from the laundry room. "Get your coat on, Craig. Let's go."

"I'm not going." He frowned.

"We need your help, Craig," she said. "I know you don't want to face all those people. But you've been a part of this from the beginning, and you have to see it through to the end."

Nelson came up behind his mother. "Yeah, suck it up, Craig."

"You watch your language, young man," said Mrs. Ark. "Now both of you get into the car. Bentley has it warmed up nicely by now. And besides, Craig, you'll be so busy you won't have time to think of yourself."

In the car, Siegfried was barking. He seemed to be urging Craig on.

Craig accompanied the family to the school. But he planned to stay out of sight as much as possible. He dreaded this day.

In contrast, the K'BeTs appeared energized by the project and had arrived at the school by ten o'clock. Preparing for a noon opening, they were too busy to pay attention to Craig. *So far, so good.*

Craig's first job was to escort Siegfried to the library where Norma Faith would conduct the pet show. Norma Faith was in her element. She had invited all pets to be outfitted in winter costumes. Siegfried sported a red ski jacket with little skis attached to the sides. Craig thought it was undignified, but Mrs. Ark delighted in making it. As he handed Siegfried over to Norma Faith, Craig said, "Now be a good dog, Siegfried, and do what Norma Faith tells you. Maybe you'll win a prize." Today, Norma Faith's hair was securely held by its scrunchy.

The school gym was decked out to resemble a winter carnival—the kind held where there was real winter. The color scheme was blue and white; cool midnight blue for winter and white for snow. Large paper murals of winter scenes were taped to the walls of the gym, as well as the halls and library. Lacy paper cutout snowflakes hung from the ceilings. Perhaps it would put people in a Christmas mood, a generous mood, Craig hoped.

A farmer loaned the club his hay wagon, which Carson was using as her booth. Her mother helped her put together a really stylish booth, looking as if it had come from snowy climes. A small staircase led into the back of the wagon. As Craig passed, he saw Carson arranging the supplies she needed to supervise groups of children in making snow globes. They would use baby food jars and a mixture of salad oil and glycerin in which to suspend silvery glitter. Little figurines were glued to the tops of the jars and when the jars were turned upside down the glitter would form a miniature snowstorm over the figurines. Craig figured that was the sort of thing girls would get a kick out of.

"Looks like you're all set, Carson," Craig said on his way to the kitchen.

"I think so." She smiled and waved at him.

Logan Raxter complimented Carson on her outstanding booth, and she glowed. Craig thought Carson looked very pretty today decked out in a dark blue velvet ice skater's costume trimmed in white fuzzy stuff.

All of the hard-working K'BeTs were stationed at their booths when Mr. Ark announced, "I'm opening the school doors to the public now, kids."

Although hundreds of tickets were sold in advance, Mrs. Day appointed a volunteer to sell more tickets at the door. Fun-seekers now arrived, and before long the entire school was a happening place.

In the kitchen, Mrs. Ark handed Craig a cake. "This is for the cake walk." He took it to Carlene in the music room, wishing he could swipe his tongue through the sugary drizzle, but he restrained himself. He stayed for a moment to take in the music and laughter. Mrs. Kerry, the music teacher, was playing the piano. Craig watched this musical chairs version of the cake walk. One chair less than the number of participants was set up in the middle of the circle of walkers. During the last round, Mrs. Wagner and tiny Steven Ludlow scrambled for the single chair. Steven won the cake.

The carnival had also taken over the lunchroom. The K'BeTs prepared plenty of food, expecting it to bring in big bucks. Hot dogs and hot wings were the mainstays of the day.

A huge pot of Cajun stew called jambalaya drew hungry people by its meaty, peppery flavored steam. Desserts covered one of the long tables and a variety of beverages another. Craig knew no one would leave the carnival hungry.

"The cake walk is a big hit," Craig reported to Mrs. Ark when he rejoined her in the lunchroom.

"I wonder who'll win my fig preserve cake?" she said.

The lunchroom doubled as the auditorium for the school, so Craig scooted into the little room behind the stage and threw his jacket onto a chair. He lingered in his hiding place, but Mr. Ark found him and directed him in adding ice to the soft drink chest. Mrs. Ark grabbed him and said, "Open these bags of plastic utensils and cups, please, Craig." Then Raxter spotted him heading for the back room and asked him to carry out some trash bags.

From the dumpster, Craig looked over at the huge pile of snow being spewed out on the playground by the snow machine. He was glad Carson got her way about that. The kids were whooping it up. A group of middle school boys brought their skateboards, minus wheels, and fashioned a ski ramp next to a small mountain of snow. They sailed through the air with all the vigor of Olympic skiers.

Gary was conducting a snowman contest. Some kids were making snow angels and others were throwing snowballs. Craig itched to join in the fun; he had never been in a snowball fight. He sighed and went back inside.

Curiosity overcame him, however, and he made his way to the gymnasium. Most of the carnival booths were set up in here, with enough variety to appeal to all age groups. The smallest kids were tumbling around in a "ball room." The balls were all white, of course. Jean insisted on that.

At one end of the gym, Shaquan directed a basketball-throwing contest. The "basketballs" were wads of white paper. Craig couldn't help but laugh at the futile attempts of the bigger boys and girls to throw the lightweight balls at the basket.

Nearby, James conducted the balloon break, where players threw darts at white balloons attached to a cork board covered in midnight blue felt.

Sarah supervised the building of gingerbread houses. The kids were using brown cardboard in place of gingerbread. Sarah included gingerbread cookies for decoration, along with white icing and sprinkles. Craig loved the smell.

Mark's ice fishing game was a variation on the usual fishing pond. Young players used little nets to scoop up bobbing plastic fish from a tub of ice cubes. The kids playing the game squealed with delight each time they "caught" a fish.

"Hey, Craig," Mark said, when he noticed Craig watching, "will you go get me some more ice cubes? Most of these have melted."

"Sure, Mark."

After taking ice cubes to Mark, Craig attempted to hide in the little room backstage again, but Mrs. Ark said, "Craig, will you go relieve Nelson for his dinner break?"

"Do I have to?" he asked. He feared no one would come near Nelson's booth if they saw him there.

"I want you to have some fun, too, Craig," Mrs. Ark said.

Huh..[VH3] I can't possibly have fun here.

He made his way through the crowds to the front hall. Nelson's booth was set up beside Carson's wagon. It was the dunk booth. Sitting precariously on a ledge over a four-foot vat of white foam cushions perched the math teacher, Miss Gimmell. She was the teacher whose car Craig had written on with a permanent marker.

Nelson rushed to Craig and handed him the three baseballs the contestants used to hit the bull's-eye that released the lever which would plunge the sitter into the pool of foam cushions. Over the noise in the hall, he shouted, "Mom said you were coming to take over. Thanks; I'll be back as soon as I grab a bite to eat."

Craig looked at the baseballs in his hand. Then he looked up and saw the smile leave Miss Gimmell's face. Craig was not the only one to see the change in the teacher's expression. He looked around and saw the crowd backing away from him. No one was going to play the game with Craig in charge. He felt heat rising from his neck to his ears. The balls fell from his hand. As he turned and charged after Nelson, he bumped into Carson. She had witnessed his humiliation.

"I have to find Nelson," Craig said.

When he reached the lunchroom, Craig saw Nelson getting a drink at the beverage table. But, instead of telling him the booth was unmanned, Craig headed backstage. He knew he should never have come today. This was bound to have happened. Now he knew where he stood with the community, he would never try to be a part of it again, ever. He found his coat in the little room and put it on to leave.

"Where are you going, Craig?" Carson followed him after he had been snubbed. He figured he should be glad.

"I'm getting away from this town."

"You know they won't let you do that. They'll find you."

"Maybe I'll find my dad first. I kinda miss him. Maybe he misses me, too."

"Maybe he doesn't want to be found."

"It doesn't matter if I ever find him. I can take care of myself."

"Craig, don't let what happened out there undo all the good the Arks have done for you. You were beginning to fit in again."

Craig felt his resolve weaken. Maybe he was being too hasty in leaving now. Maybe... At that moment a loud disturbance in the lunchroom broke into his thoughts. He heard the crash of a table, laughter, barking, and voices. "Siegfried!" " Siegfried!" " Siegfried!"

Craig and Carson rushed from the little room to the stage. The big tub of jambalaya lay turned over on the floor, giving off a spicy fragrance. A parade of yelping dogs lapped up the jambalaya, but not Siegfried. It looked as if Siegfried had run away from Norma Faith and the pet show. He leaped onto his ole pal, Craig.

Craig, Siegfried, and Carson, fell to the floor in a heap, caught up in the hilarity surrounding them.

No one had been hurt by splashing stew. Everyone within swiping distance grabbed napkins and dishrags and pitched into the cleanup. Others helped Norma Faith round up the stampede and herd the dogs back to the library.

Sitting on the floor with Siegfried, Craig hugged the dog. Carson reached over and stroked Siegfried's head.

"He has canine ESP," she said.

Craig nodded. Not for the first time, he wondered how Siegfried knew he needed him. "I guess I'll stay a while longer."

After the spilled food was cleaned, the reveling resumed.

In the early December dusk, Mr. Ark called the merry-makers outside. The snow machine was turned off, and the frozen kids who had been playing in snow, joined everyone else on the front lawn of the school. Craig went, too.

The committee left the most beautiful surprise for last. At Mr. Ark's signal, hundreds of lights in the trees and bushes lit up. Tiny, white bits of crystals sparkled in the fading twilight. The school was transformed into a winter wonderland. Craig saw enraptured expressions on many faces and heard lots of "Oooh's" and "Aaah's" and "Isn't this spectacular!"

Ascending the front steps, Mr. Ark got everyone's attention. "I want to say just a few words, folks." Craig slipped behind the bushes beside the steps. He didn't want to be recognized.

"First," said Mr. Ark, "thanks, K'BeTs, for all your fine, hard work on behalf of the injured tree." The crowd applauded and shouted.

"There has been an incredible outpouring of love for the old tree," resumed Mr. Ark. "It has brought this community together in friendship as I have never witnessed in my life before. I don't think I have ever seen so many people pull together for a common cause."

Mr. Ark laughed. "This day has been a great success. And lots of thanks go to Mrs. Day, the club's sponsor, and the parents of the K'BeTs, and to Mrs. Kassi, the school principal, and all of you who participated in this fundraiser." The crowd applauded again. "And raise funds we did! David Larsen, come on up here with me." Mr. Ark waited until the loan officer from the bank joined him on the top step. The two men shook hands. "I have here a check which I am now handing to Mr. Larsen in repayment of the loan the bank provided for the therapy to the tree."

You'd think he was paying off the national debt, by the sound of the cheering.

Mr. Larsen thanked Mr. Ark. "If I may, I would like to quote the poet, H. F. Chorley, and propose a toast:

>   'Then here's to the oak, the brave old oak,
>   Who stands in his pride alone!
>   And still flourish he a hale green tree
>   When a hundred years are gone!'"

Mr. Larsen waved the check in the air as he descended the steps.

When the clamor subsided, Mr. Ark continued. "And let's have a round of applause for Logan Raxter, the best tree man in six counties!" More loud appreciation erupted from the crowd, and those standing near Raxter clapped him on the back and shook his hand.

Then Craig watched Mr. Ark wave good-bye to the assembly with a smile on his face and turn away with tears in his eyes.

Chapter Fifteen

> *"Just as the twig is bent, the tree's inclined."*
> Alexander Pope

The rest of the winter passed routinely. Short cold spells plunged the thermometer into the freeing zone but the heater kept the interior of the ICU warm.

Craig piled more mulch around the base of the giant tree. If only wishing could make it well. If only… If only Craig could turn back the clock. What had he said before he revved up the chain saw: "Who needs it?" Now he knew. *He* needed the tree. Raxter needed it. The K'BeTs needed it. The Arks needed it. At last he admitted to himself a connection to the tree. *I guess we're hitched up for life,* he told himself grudgingly. Raxter had been right.

Craig had been trying to "mend" the tree as he thought the judge meant him to do. Now he felt secure enough in his life to try to mend some of the other wounds he inflicted. He wrote letters of apology to the math teacher and the art teacher.

Craig enjoyed a natural-feeling relationship with the Ark family, especially the times when he and Nelson studied together at the kitchen table. Siegfried even gave Craig his favorite squeaky toy, a plastic mailman.

When Mrs. Ark poured over seed catalogs, Craig sat beside her on the sofa and they discussed spring plantings.

One frosty day, Craig helped Mr. Ark clean the big fish tank in the living room. "I've been thinking about putting a koi pond in the butterfly garden," Mr. Ark said.

"That's a great idea. Could I help?"

"I could sure use another hand. By the way, Craig, thanks for taking over the car washing duty."

Craig's face grew warm. "Oh, sure."

"Hey, Craig," called Nelson. "When you're done with the fish tank, let's go up and play a video game." All they had these days were old games.

Craig followed Nelson up to his room and challenged him to a double-controlled game of "Silent Hill." They let all the stops out.

"I've got you now," yelled Craig.

"Oh, no, you haven't," Nelson yelled just as loudly.

Craig groaned as Nelson's character pounded his character, then the tables were turned and Nelson groaned. Back and forth the game went, and in his imagination Craig could be strong and whole and a hero.

On Super Bowl Sunday, Craig sat with the family in the living room and rooted for the Tampa Bay Buccaneers. A few times, Mrs. Ark took Craig, Carson, Nelson and Jean to a movie in the city. Craig continued to see Mrs. Dayton on a regular basis.

* * * *

Carson still came home with the boys to study at least

once a week. She and Craig had become good friends. One day as they strolled through Mrs. Ark's garden, Craig said, "I have a secret, Carson."

"Do you want to tell me?"

"I wrote an apology to Miss Gimmell and to the art teacher."

Carson smiled at him. "Thanks for telling me, Craig. I think that was the right thing to do."

Taking Carson's hand, Craig was happy about this special connection.

Life appeared normal except for Mr. Ark's long absences. He assured the boys he was working late at the store, but he could have carpeted the whole county by now. He couldn't be doing the books, because Mrs. Ark still went into the store to do the bookkeeping. And all of the hurricane flood damage was cleaned up. After returning from out of town trips, Mr. Ark never talked about his activities. Sometimes he seemed worried and at other times he seemed excited.

Whatever his secret was, it baffled Craig.

* * * *

For the most part, Craig concentrated his attention on the sick tree. Every day he checked the soil around the feeder trees for the proper amount of moisture.

"How much fertilizer today, Mr. Raxter?" he might ask.

Or Raxter might say, "Adjust the spray nozzle to a gentle spray, Craig."

They joked around some. One time Craig said, "Mr.

Raxter, I know another way to get the elephant into the tree."

"How's that?"

"I would make him wait till after winter and spring up."

"Ooooh! That's pretty lame," said Raxter, but he laughed any way. "You know, Craig, you're getting pretty good at keeping all these machines running. You have a mechanical gift." Praise from Raxter was better than chocolate.

When they checked the grafted connections, Craig made the necessary repairs as easily as Raxter. They replaced some small dead trees with new saplings.

Raxter told Craig about his work in the city as Urban Arborist. His responsibilities included caring for trees on city property and advising citizens on tree removal and replacement. "Tree diseases give me the most trouble," he told Craig. "I hate it when we get a blight—like the Southern pine beetles on the loblolly pines. We had to destroy hundreds of trees so the blight wouldn't spread; we had no other choice." Raxter had a great respect for trees. He was a big man with a big love for big plants.

"Are you a tree hugger, Mr. Raxter?" Craig asked.

Raxter laughed and nodded. "I guess I am, Craig. Where did you hear that expression? It's not always used as a compliment."

"Nelson read a book about a little girl in India, named Aani, who led her whole village in hugging their trees so they wouldn't be cut down. He said it was a true story."

"I believe it. I've read stories about people who risk their lives for their trees."

* * * *

Craig knew there were other tree lovers, like the ones pictured in *The Sierra Magazine*. One evening when he and Nelson lay on their stomachs in front of the fireplace, enjoying the aroma of the wood fire, Nelson showed him an article about people who hauled sleeping bags up into the branches of tall trees and camped out up there. The pictures were awesome.

"Let's try it sometime," Craig said.

"Okay," said Nelson. "Let's wait till warmer weather, though."

Chapter Sixteen

"One impulse from a vernal wood
May teach you more of man,
Of moral evil and of good,
Than all the ages can."
William Wordsworth

On one especially mild day in February, Craig went out to check on the tree. Approaching it, he was caught in a blizzard of brown leaves. He looked up and was alarmed to realize the canopy looked skimpy. *I just noticed. The tree is not doing well at all. Have I been concentrating so hard on helping the tree that I couldn't see what's really happening to it?* The thought made him sick. A fearful premonition blacked out his vision—for a moment, he saw no leaves at all on the tree.

Nelson followed Craig into the ICU, twirling his basketball. "Sure smells musty in here," he said. "Can you do anything about that?"

"I don't know what else to do." Craig forced his words through tight lips. He clenched his fists. "I've done everything Mr. Raxter told me to. He's done everything he can think of. Now we're just waiting."

"Don't look so desperate, Craig. The tree looks pretty good, considering. I think all these little feeder trees are really helping."

Nelson! With his enthusiasm.

"Nelson, you are so thick." Craig turned on Nelson. "What do you know? You always think everything is going to turn out fine. Your life is fine. Well, not everybody's life is fine. And not everything turns out fine."

"Gee, Craig, you always let everything get to you. You said there's nothing you can do right now. How about coming out and shooting some baskets with me?"

Craig surprised himself and Nelson by guffawing loudly. How could he stay mad at Nelson? Siegfried barked— this time happily. "You're too much, Nelson." Craig chuckled and squatted down to scratch Siegfried around the neck. He looked up at Nelson and smiled. "Thanks, I'd like to shoot some baskets with you. This tree is getting me down."

The two boys and dog ran over to the garage where the basketball hoop was attached above the doors. The driveway was a good solid surface for bouncing and dribbling the ball. Craig's height was little advantage in the face of Nelson's agility and speed. The score was pretty even. Siegfried ran back and forth barking, not realizing he was in the way. But the boys didn't scold him. "Siegfried thinks he's playing, too," said Craig.

"I'm winded," said Nelson after a while.

"Yeah, me, too. Let's take a break." Craig took some deep breaths and bounced the ball on the cement. "Hey, that was fun. And my leg didn't hold me back too much."

"I didn't see it hold you back at all," Nelson said.

Wounds

"You're nearly back to normal."

"Just about," said Craig, "but Dr. Leopold says I'll always have a limp. Anyway, I've been meaning to thank you for helping me with my school work."

"Aw… I'm glad your grades have improved. Mom says you needed a chance to catch up to where you were before your mother died."

"Don't go there, Nelson," Craig warned.

"I'm not. It's just that I don't understand why you won't talk about your mother. She was a nice lady. It isn't your fault she died."

Craig's face turned hard as he felt his heart almost stop. He slammed the basketball into Nelson's stomach. "Yes, it is," he shouted.

Nelson's mouth dropped open, the ball rolling onto the grass. Craig left him that way and headed into the woods. Dodging trees and brambles, he ran to clear his mind of thoughts of his mother's death. The guilt was more than he could bear.

Craig returned when red streaks of sunset faded in the darkening sky. He knew he could count on Nelson not to tattle. He sat quietly through dinner, picking at his tuna casserole while [BB4]family chatter wove a net of peacefulness around him. A thought came to him like a flicker from the shadows that this would be the only time he would ever be part of a real family again. He felt calm and resigned to his fate. One thing he knew for sure—if the tree died, too, he would run away for good.

107

Chapter Seventeen

*"For I must to the greenwood go;
Alone, a banished man."*
Anonymous

Craig looked out the window of the school bus at the gathering clouds and swaying trees. The driver turned the headlights on to cut through the dusk. A spring storm was threatening to erupt. Darkness in the middle of the day was eerie, adding feelings of impending disaster to Craig's gloomy spirits. *It's like being wrapped in the devil's cloak.*

Why am I in such a foul mood? The spring had been so beautiful. He helped Mrs. Ark replace the camellias alongside the road. They worked cheerfully side by side, laughing at the cats sprawled belly-up in the sun. Buds were setting in the rose bushes.

Craig really enjoyed helping Mr. Ark and Nelson put in the koi pond. He could dig and shovel dirt with the best of them. Hard work cleared his mind of "confused thinking," as Judge Borowsky predicted. When the big goldfish were in place, he and Nelson lay on their stomachs on the rounded wooden bridge and watched them dart in and out of the grass like big Spanish doubloons. Butterflies swarmed among the milkweeds.

Yes, everything was thriving except the tree.

Now, as Craig and Nelson got off the school bus, the wind tore at their shirts.

Hunched against the bluster, the boys raced to the porch. A strong gust slammed the door behind them. Laughing, Nelson said, "We barely made it."

Mrs. Ark helped the boys off with their backpacks. "I'm glad you boys didn't get wet," she said. Craig was expecting her to offer them a hot drink with their after school snack. But instead she said, "Nelson, run along into the kitchen, please; Craig has a visitor."

"I'll take your backpack, Craig," said Nelson as he departed.

"Is it Mrs. Dayton?" Who else could it be?

"No, it isn't." Mrs. Ark gently took Craig by the arm and steered him into the living room.

Mr. Ark stood by the curio cabinet.

In the middle of the room, his lanky arms moving restlessly, stood Craig's dad, Charlie Reeves. He took one lurching step toward Craig, and then stopped. His thin face was full of expectancy. His eyes begged for—what? For forgiveness? For understanding? For love?

"God, I've missed you, son." His eyes looked watery and he swallowed hard.

Craig was so stunned he couldn't move. *It's all over. They'll make me go back. And I'll get beaten up and go hungry and I'll never get to play video games again.* He twisted out of Mrs. Ark's grasp.

"It's all right, Craig," she said. "Stay and listen to what

your dad has to say."

"Craig…" said Charlie as he came forward with outstretched arms.

"Don't touch me…! You left me all alone. Where have you been? Why didn't you call or write? You've been in jail, haven't you?"

"Craig, give me a chance to explain."

"You have a lot to explain." Craig spoke the bitter words with sarcasm.

"Mr. Ark has helped me, son. I've been trying to get myself together. I want us to have a normal life again."

"You think you can come back here and everything will be normal? Well, things weren't normal before you ran away. And things will never be all right again. Not with Mom gone."

Craig burst into tears and covered his face and his dad came to him and wrapped his arms around him. Charlie was crying, too. They clung to each other, sobbing, until Craig came to his senses and remembered who this man was. This man abandoned him. Hurt him. Left him to bear the guilt of his mother's death alone. Craig wrenched himself out of his dad's arms and backed away. He frowned and swiped his face with his fist.

"I've done terrible things because of you. I'm better off without you!" *That's right, Craig; keep on hurting people. That's all you know.*

Craig could tell his words wounded his dad. Charlie looked from Craig down to the floor and took a handkerchief from his pocket. He blew his nose. But he didn't hit Craig.

"You're still mad at me," Charlie said. "And I don't blame you. You miss your mom. I know. I missed her so much I couldn't take care of you after she died. But things are different now."

Mr. Ark came forward. "Let's all sit down and talk things over. We have a lot to tell you, Craig."

Mrs. Ark twisted the knob that brightened the lights of the chandelier because the storm clouds had plunged the room into a well of darkness. The howling of the wind screamed over the hard raindrops hitting the house like pellets from a hundred BB guns.

"I'll bring in some drinks," Mrs. Ark said.

Charlie and Mr. Ark went around the coffee table to sit on the sofa. Craig sat in the same chair he sat in the day Carson invited him to join in the K'BeTs' planning session. Siegfried sank down with his head on Craig's foot.

Mrs. Ark passed around cups of steaming mugs in silence and sat down.

Charlie looked at Mr. Ark.

"Craig," Mr. Ark said, his voice searching for a light-hearted effect, "doesn't your dad look good and healthy? I know you can tell he's sober."

Craig didn't say anything. *Yeah, you look better than you did the last time I saw you* .[VH5] *Clean, shaved, new clothes. Not stinking of whiskey.* "But, for how long?" he asked aloud.

"I've kicked the drinking, son. Believe me; I've been

sober for six months."

"Your dad has been in rehab, Craig," said Mrs. Ark. "My husband has been visiting him and giving him encouragement." That explained Mr. Ark's mysterious disappearances.

"And that's not all," said Charlie. "The Arks paid for the rehab place and for my training. I took my GED test—I've got a high school diploma."

"That's why we ran out of money and couldn't pay for the treatment for the tree," Mr. Ark said. "But the town sure came through in the pinch."

"I still don't see why you didn't contact me."

"Craig, to tell the truth, we weren't sure I would ever be able to get you back."

"We didn't want you to get your hopes up, honey," Mrs. Ark said.

"We wanted to keep you as our own boy if your dad's rehab didn't work out," Mr. Ark said.

"I want to come clean with you, Craig," Charlie said. "I want you to understand why I was drinking so heavy after your mother died." A look of shame came over Charlie's face. "You were right, son; I was in jail for a while. Rod Boyle, the deputy sheriff, hunted me down the night after we both ran away. I was so full of guilt, I couldn't stand it. It scared me what I was doing. I was afraid that I would kill you like I killed your mother."

Craig interrupted his father. "What do you mean, you killed her? You didn't kill Mom."

"I know that now. But then I thought I caused her death. Do you remember the day your mom got hurt?"

Craig leaned over with the palms of his hands covering his eyes and rested his elbows on his knees. He might as well let his dad talk before he told him the truth—he, Craig, was responsible for his mother's death. He leaned against the back of the chair, listening.

Above the noisy storm, Charlie told his story. "That day I was in a hurry to leave for work; I was putting on a new roof for the Webers. It was my first big job and I was anxious to get it done right. Our whole future depended on it. Well, I forgot my lunch." The way Charlie shook his head showed his annoyance with himself.

"When Julia realized I left my lunch bag on the kitchen table, she grabbed it and decided to bring it to me. You had already gone to school. She caught a bus going toward town and rode to the cut-off to the Weber place. It wasn't a far walk from there. She was wearing an old pair of sneakers."

Craig knew the Weber house—a rambling old farm house reached by a shady avenue of pecan trees.

"I had started tearing off the old roof; throwing tarpaper and rotten boards down on the ground. I was going to clean it all up later. There wadn't anybody else there except me. Julia walked around the house till she found me at the back. She told me why she came, and I told her to put the lunch in my truck. I was glad she brought it to me because I was working up a real big appetite. She left and I went back to work. I was makin' a racket and I didn't hear her yell when she stepped on that rusty roofing nail."

At the thought of his mother experiencing pain, Craig sat forward and shook his head. He didn't want to have to remember this, but he merely sucked in his breath as his dad continued his story.

"Yeah, I know it's hard to think about, son, but she was one tough lady. She sat down and pulled that nail right out of her shoe and her foot. It wasn't bleedin' bad, so she put some tissues in her shoe and caught the next bus home."

Craig pictured his mother, tall and slim, brave and plucky.

"When she got home, she washed her foot but she didn't have any mercurochrome. She didn't think about going to the doctor. When she told me, I didn't think much about it; except I was sorry she got hurt.

"The next few days, I didn't know it was gettin' worse."

Craig remembered his mother hobbling around, favoring the foot, but he had not known her condition was getting worse, either.

"When her foot swelled so bad she couldn't get her shoe on, I got concerned. I told her she should have gone to the doctor before now. She said she had more important things to do with the money."

Oh, yeah. Craig covered his face. *She had something real important to do with the money.*

"By then she had a pretty high fever," said Charlie. "I decided to take her to the emergency room. Well, you know, because you went with us."

Craig nodded his head.

"Dr. Leopold said it was some real bad infection—sudy-something."

"I remember," Mr. Ark said. *"Pseudomonas aeurqinosa."*

"That's right," said Charlie, shaking his head. "We had never even heard of it. The doctor said he might have saved her if she had come in right after the accident. It was them old sneakers that had the germs in them. He said rubber soles are full of germs.

"She would have gone to the doctor if we had medical insurance. I was planning to get some as soon as my business started making some money. Then when she died, I blew it. I quit working and started drinking."

Craig wished his dad would stop talking. This wasn't doing anybody any good.

"In rehab, I learned it was an accident," Charlie said. "I don't need to feel guilty any more. What I need to do is get on with my life and take care of you, Craig. I was just thinking of myself. But now I have good prospects, thanks to Mr. Ark." He glanced at Mr. Ark, who smiled back. "As soon as I get a job, I'll be able to pay Mr. Ark rent on our little house and soon I'll have enough to get us a few nice things. Well, what do you say, son? Talk to me."

Craig had sat through his father's confession listening quietly but with his teeth gritted, clenching his fists. Now he sat up briskly.

Jumping to his feet, Craig faced his father squarely. "You've wasted your guilt for nothing. You drank yourself stupid for nothing. You didn't kill Mom; I did. What do you think she was saving her money for? She was going to get me a video game player. If it hadn't been for me, she would have gone to the doctor and been treated for that crazy disease. I'm the one who's to blame." Craig jabbed himself in the chest with his thumb. "And I've done other terrible things because I'm a rotten person!"

He saw the shock on his father's face, but he didn't care.

Craig turned and ran from the room.

Chapter Eighteen

*"We'll to the woods no more,
The laurels are all cut."*
Theodore de Banville

A storm inside Craig raged more fiercely than the one beating against the house. It thundered against his dad's confession. It washed away the generosity of the Arks. The lightening of his guilt illuminated all his transgressions and blinded him to mercy and forgiveness. The storm threatened to destroy his life.

As Craig stumbled into the kitchen, followed by Siegfried, the astonished voices behind him receded. Craig started to say goodbye to Nelson, but decided to leave without a word.

If Craig left by the back door, the wind would rush through the house, giving him away. Instead, he left through the laundry room leading to the garage. He barely noticed as Siegfried slipped through. Craig carefully closed the laundry room door.

Where could he go? Where could he hide until the storm blew over? He thought of the ICU. That might be the first place they would look, but he could stay there for a few minutes to collect his thoughts. He pushed the button and opened the garage door.

From the shelter of the garage, Craig looked toward the tree. Here was all the proof he needed, if he needed proof of his villainy. Most of the ICU was gone—ripped apart like a soggy tissue. Not a single leaf hung from any branch of the tree.

He made a little tent of his hands over his eyes to protect them from the pelting rain and ran to the tree. The dream he had in the ER came back to him and once again he saw the tree—barren, leafless in the center of a great vast desert. But, it was no longer a dream.

His imagination carried him above the tree from where it seemed he could see himself and the whole world—green and blue. White flowers on Mrs. Ark's dogwood trees. Pink azaleas. Red tulips. Everywhere there were specks of color. But not here. Here, where the giant oak should have been a mass of vibrant green, there was only the brown of decay.

Feeling the weight of the sky on his shoulders, Craig dropped to his knees. The cold dampness of the earth seeped into his jeans and crept up to his chest. A strangled cry escaped his tightened throat.

Craig looked out through a film of tears and saw not just the tree; he saw the truth. The tree was dead.

He sprang up and ran to the tree, avoiding shards of the ruined ICU. He tried to encircle the huge trunk with his arms. The rough bark scratched his cheek. Sobs shook his body and he screamed, "No, No." Somewhere deep inside his broken heart, his voice whispered, "I did this; I killed you, too."

Craig felt a hand on his shoulder. He turned and saw

Nelson. Nelson shouted against the storm. "Come back into the house, Craig." Siegfried barked, looking from one boy to the other. No use trying to explain to Nelson. Craig lurched up and backed toward the forest, looking down at Siegfried.

Over the noise of the wind, he said, "Are you coming with me, Siegfried?" Siegfried looked confused. He trotted a few steps toward Craig then stopped. He turned and looked at Nelson. Then back at Craig. His decision made, he returned to Nelson. Craig said, "Okay; have it your way." He wheeled around and headed into the woods alone.

The going was hard. He couldn't run. He had to push against the wind. Under the noise he faintly heard Nelson calling: "Don't go, Craig!"

But he shoved on. Where was he going? How could he evade capture? He needed help. He would double back and head for the road to town. Who did he know in that direction who would help him? Carson. He would go to her. She would help him get out of town without being spotted.

It seemed like a pretty good plan. That's what he would do.

Twigs and leaves flew about in great confusion. A limb broke off from a tree to Craig's right with a sharp crack. Short-stemmed palmetto fronds scraped at his legs with their pointed daggers. A great gust of wind howled at him and knocked him against a tree. He steadied himself, holding on to the tree until the wind abated. Time to start circling back toward the road.

Craig felt a pain in his ankle. He looked down to see

Siegfried latched onto his leg. "Let go, Siegfried! What are you doing? Did you decide to go with me after all?" Siegfried let go and barked. Craig felt the back of his leg; the skin was barely scratched. He squatted down and rubbed Siegfried's back. "It might be a little harder going with you, but I don't care. Let's go."

But Siegfried turned and headed back toward the house. "What's wrong now? If you're trying to get me to go back with you, *forget it*. Now, we don't have time to *waste*. Come on!" He resumed his journey, but again Siegfried gripped his leg. "Stop it, Siegfried. Why are you acting so crazy?"

Siegfried barked frantically and ran short distances toward home then back to Craig. "Hey, are you trying to tell me something? Who do you think you are, Lassie?"

Craig looked back toward the tree. He had come less than a hundred yards; the tree was still visible. Through sheets of rain, he saw a fallen limb on the ground. [BB6]He hadn't heard the crash. Something red was on the ground by the limb. Nelson had been wearing a red shirt. Was that Nelson lying there under the limb?

"Is Nelson hurt, Siegfried? Is that why you came for me? Go back and get Mr. Ark, Siegfried. I can't go. Don't you see? If I go back I'll lose my head start. I can't be looking out for that kid. I have to look out for number one." *Like when my mom died. All I could think about was getting a game station. But what if Nelson dies? It will be my fault again.*

Siegfried continued to look up at Craig, yipping now

and then.

Craig thought of the kindness of the Arks. "They've been good to me. And so has Carson and Mr. Raxter. I've got friends here. You're right, Siegfried. I can't let Nelson *die*—even if my dad beats me to death."

Back through the woods the boy and dog ran, Craig limping badly. Craig found Nelson pinned under the fallen limb. "Nelson, Nelson! Are you alive?" Craig was afraid to touch the still, unconscious body.

Water splashing onto Nelson's face revived him. He uttered a faint, "Help."

"I'm right here, Nelson. I'm going to help you. Are you conscious? Can you scoot out from under the limb if I lift it?"

"Yeah," Nelson said.

Craig tugged on the limb holding Nelson down. It budged a little, but not enough.

Using strength he didn't know he had, Craig strained at the limb. Getting better traction with his feet, he lifted the limb a few inches. "Now, Nelson."

Nelson squeezed his eyes shut, strained and pushed with his feet, grunting. In a moment, he was out from under the limb. He relaxed from the tension and passed one hand over his face. But the other arm lay at an awkward angle, blood soaking the shirt sleeve.

Craig lowered the limb back to the ground and took some deep breaths. "Can you stand if I help you?"

"I don't think so."

"I'll go get your dad."

Craig headed for the house. His concern for Nelson chased all other thoughts from his mind.

Craig rushed through the garage into the laundry room. Through the kitchen. Then down the hall. At the entrance to the living room he halted, water dripping from his hair and clothes. Everyone stopped talking and looked at him.

"Nelson's been hurt."

The news roused the group. "What happened?"

"Where is he?"

"A limb from the tree fell on him."

"I'll come, too," Charlie said, following the Arks and Craig outside.

Everybody was talking at once.

"We didn't know you boys had gone outside."

"What were you doing out here?"

Mrs. Ark knelt beside her son. "Are you hurt badly, Nelson?"

"My arm's broken."

"Oh, my baby."

Mr. and Mrs. Ark helped Nelson to his feet.

"Let's get out from under this tree before more branches fall."

"Back to the Emergency Room," Craig said.

Chapter Nineteen

"A tree is known by its fruit; a man by his deeds. A good deed is never lost."

Saint Basil

When the group arrived at the Emergency Room, Dr. Leopold quickly attended to Nelson's wound. Mr. and Mrs. Ark stayed in the treatment cubicle while the doctor set and cast the broken arm.

Craig waited with his dad on the chairs lined against the wall opposite the treatment room. *It's like it was the night I was here—only now we're switched. I was in the exam room and Nelson was out here with his parents. I wonder what he was thinking? He must have hated me for cutting the tree. But he didn't act like it. I hated myself, though. Now I've gone and done it again. Nelson wouldn't be here if it wasn't for me.*

Now that Nelson was alive and all right, Craig began to wish he hadn't come back, after all. He had lost his chance to escape, and the new guilt of Nelson's injury was added to all his other misdeeds. He slipped over a seat, putting some distance between himself and his dad, leaned over with his face in his hands, and let out a great sigh.

"Don't you worry none about Nelson, son; he's going to be fine."

Craig stiffened under the light touch of his dad's hand

on his bent back. Jerking away from his dad, Craig said, "That's not it. Can't you see? I nearly got Nelson killed. Mom; the tree; Nelson. I hurt everybody. I want to get away from here."

"You can't get away from yourself, Craig. Now, you have made some bad choices. From now on you must make the right choices. That was a brave thing you did lifting a heavy branch off of Nelson. He coudda bled to death. What were you two doing out there, anyway?"

Craig looked down at the floor, his hands dangling between his knees. He saw a little puddle of water where his shoes had dripped on the square tiles. What would his dad do to him if he came clean?

"I was leaving town. Nelson was trying to talk me out of it."

His dad didn't take him by the scruff of the neck or slap him or use foul language.

"Craig, this running away has got to stop—for both of us. You don't solve anything that way."

Craig sat silently taking in what his dad was saying. Then Charlie added, "I'm going to help you, son."

Craig sat up straight and looked directly into his dad's eyes. He could hardly believe what he was hearing; or seeing. Charlie looked so clear-eyed, so sincere, so knowing. "You're going to help me?" asked Craig. "You're not going to beat me up anymore?"

"That's all behind us, son. And you're going to help me. You're my whole reason to live now. If there's one thing

I've learned it's you can't go it alone. We've got friends we can depend on." Charlie's voice became low and slow. "But you've got to forgive me, Craig."

Craig looked down at his hands in his lap. He reached down and rubbed the wounded leg— a constant reminder of his own guilt. "I forgive you, Dad," he said, "but I'm the one who's caused all the trouble."

"Then you're going to have to forgive yourself, son."

Chapter Twenty

> *"A good word is as a good tree--
> its roots are firm, and its
> branches are in heaven."*
> QIR' AN, XIV: 2 7-33

"Help me drag this limb into the woods, Craig," called Charlie. It was the day following the big storm and Craig and his dad were helping clear away the rubble.

Nelson sent for the K'BeTs, but, excused from work, he sat on the bench in the rose garden, wrapped in a blanket. Everyone was working hard. Siegfried ran all around.

Craig called Logan Raxter, too.

* * * *

The previous evening, everyone had returned from the Emergency Room damp and tired. They all changed into dry clothes, and Mrs. Ark put Nelson to bed. He looked drowsy when Craig went into his room. "I'm sorry you got hurt, Nelson."

Nelson's good hand stroked Siegfried who was curled up on his bed. "Don't worry about it, Craig; Dr. Leopold gave me some pain medicine. I'll be all right. Hey—I'm glad we got to you before you got away." Siegfried flapped his ears. "You're not going to run away anymore, are you?"

"No. I've got it all worked out with my dad."

"Good."

Craig looked down at the floor. "There's something I want say. I don't think I ever told you how sorry I am about the tree."

"I already knew it, Craig." Nelson yawned. "I could tell. It wasn't just punishment."

"Anyway. I apologize."

"Okay. Do you want to sign my cast?"

"Really?" Craig hadn't expected that. "You want me to?"

After the signing, Craig left Nelson and Siegfried to go to sleep and joined the adults in the kitchen. Outside, the sound of the storm had died down; people could now talk without shouting.

"What a day," said Mr. Ark with a sigh.

"I am so glad it's over." Mrs. Ark poured hot chocolate into mugs, the fragrant steam pleasant and cozy. She sliced cheese for sandwiches, too.

But it isn't quite over. [VH7]

Apologizing to Nelson created a good feeling in Craig—a small seed of forgiveness now sprouting into life. Craig wanted to fertilize the new feeling and help it grow.

"Uh." Craig looked into his mug and spoke. "I'm sorry...I'm sorry I killed the tree."

Mrs. Ark stopped slicing. Mr. Ark's mug suspended half way to his mouth. Charlie sloshed cocoa on the table. Craig looked at the Arks. The silence deepened. Would they forgive him?

"Craig," said Mr. Ark at length. "It took a lot of

courage for you to say that."

Mrs. Ark came around the table and hugged Craig. "The tree's injury will be with you always. That's a lot of punishment for you to have to carry around. But don't let it hold you back from being a good boy from now on." She released him and resumed serving food.

"And don't listen to people who throw it up at you," said his dad.

"I will try to be good from now on." Craig looked at Mr. Ark.

"Craig, I'm hurt. I admit that," Mr. Ark said. "We can't erase the past. But, we can forge a new friendship… I forgive you."

The word Craig longed to hear—forgive—lifted a weight from his heart. *At last, I can forgive myself.* [VH8]

Craig went to sleep that night with a lighter heart than he had felt in a long time. Charlie slept in the other bed in the guest room.

* * * *

Now as Craig helped with the cleanup, he thought: *My life is getting cleaned up, too.* The months of worry and anticipation were behind him. Craig could concentrate on the future. He had the support of the Arks and encouragement from his dad. He could move mountains!

But when he tried to pick up an end of the big limb, Craig laughed out loud. He couldn't muster strength to lift the heavy bough. "I don't know how I did this yesterday."

Raxter approached. "Let me give you a hand there,

Craig. Is this your dad?"

Craig was proud to have an ally like Logan Raxter, but he wished he could be as proud of his dad. "Dad, this is Mr. Raxter—I told you about him."

Charlie lowered his end of the limb and came around with his hand extended. "Glad to meet you, Mr. Raxter. I appreciate what you've done for my boy."

Raxter took Charlie's hand. "Craig is going to grow up to be a fine man, Mr. Reeves. He's learned a lot from this experience. And call me Logan."

"Likewise; call me Charlie."

"Is this the limb that fell on Nelson?"

"Yes, sir," said Craig.

Raxter stepped back and took a long look up at the stricken tree. And Craig looked up to where the washed-clean blue sky showed through the empty spaces where leaves should have been.

Raxter released a heavy sigh. "We did all we could, Craig. It's a sad day. Lots of people worked hard to prevent this. But nature can take only so much of a beating. The old tree put up a good fight." He turned and looked at Craig.

I have to say it one more time. If I don't, it will be between us forever—the ghost of the tree standing as solid as dead wood. "Mr. Raxter, I'm really sorry I killed the tree. What I did was wrong."

"What you did was wrong, yes. And you've learned a mighty hard lesson. We couldn't reroute the tree's life-giving sap, but we sure rerouted your life. I can see the change in you; you've been living your apology." He turned to Craig's dad. "Let's get rid of this debris, Charlie."

The K'BeTs were dismantling what was left of the ICU. While Raxter and Charlie hauled the big limb into the woods, Craig joined the kids.

"Is there a hammer I can use?"

"Here's one," said Carson. "And we need the ladder so we can get to the plastic that's nailed to the tree."

"I'll bring one from the shed," Mr. Ark said. "Hey, Shaquan, how about giving me a hand with the ladder?"

Mrs. Ark brought out lemonade and banana bread for everyone.

"Hey, y'all!" Nelson huddled on his bench. "Come over here."

"What do you need?" Jean asked, running over.

"How would you guys like to sign my cast?" Nelson offered Jean a blue magic marker.

Chapter Twenty-One

*"Today I have grown taller
from walking with the trees."*
Karle Wilson Baker

"Hey, Craig, can you come over to my house?"

Craig was surprised to hear Nelson's voice on the phone. The two boys had not been together much in the past six weeks. Craig and his dad had been busily putting their little house to rights, as well as mending their battered relationship. Charlie was true to his word; the drinking was behind him and he worked hard every day.

Judge Borowsky gave Craig and Charlie permission to resume living together on the recommendation of Mrs. Dayton. Their counselor assured them in time they would make a new life for themselves.

"How can life ever be normal without Mom?" Craig had asked. The counselor advised him and Charlie to create "a new kind of normal." They were trying to do that with all their might.

"Yeah, Nelson," Craig now replied into the phone. "I'll be right over."

Craig took the forest trail to visit Nelson. This time was so different from that day when he fled his home. He felt no malice. Today he enjoyed his surroundings. The sky was clear, the ground was dry, and the air was a-thrill with flying creatures. Birdsong and the fragrance of wild honeysuckle floated on the light breeze.

Emerging from the forest, Craig saw Nelson shooting baskets beside the garage with Siegfried chasing the bouncing ball. "Hey, Nelson! What's up?"

Nelson stretched his arm over his head. "This is what's up. The cast's off."

"That's great. Hi ya, Siegfried."

Siegfried ran over to greet his old friend, tail wagging, and Craig stooped to scratch him around the ruff.

"I was hoping you could stay and play some basketball," said Nelson.

"Sure thing; toss me the ball."

The boys and Siegfried played basketball like three scrappy pups worrying the same piece of rawhide.

"We both ought to try out for basketball when we get to high school," Nelson said.

"I don't think they would let me play," Craig said.

"I don't see why not. Your limp isn't that bad."

"Well, I might at least try out."

"Another thing," Nelson said. "The K'BeTs want to know if you will join the club."

"Are you serious?" Distracted, Craig let the basketball run past him. It rolled in the direction of the oak.

Craig reached the ball and stooped down. "Hey, Nelson! Look at this. Here's a perfectly healthy acorn. What do you say we plant it?"

Wounds

"You mean, like the old tree will go on living because of its baby?"

"Yeah, I guess that's what I mean."

"Great idea. Dad said he's going to have the dead tree removed and build something nice with it, maybe the skateboard ramp. Let's do it! I'll get a trowel." Nelson started for the shed.

"No need, Nelson." Craig laughed. "Siegfried already dug a hole."

So the three of them—Craig, Nelson, and Siegfried—planted the acorn together in the shadow of the ancestral oak.

> *"If a tree dies, plant another*
> *in its place."*
> Linnaeus

Wounds Acknowledgments

The author would like to acknowledge the help and cooperation of the publishers and agents who granted permission for the use of the following quotes:

Random House, Inc. for the poem, "Woods," by W. H. Auden: the NA print rights;
The Wylie agency, for the poem, "Woods," by W. H. Auden: the UK print rights and the ebook rights.

Random House, Inc. for the line from THE LORAX, by Dr. Seuss.

Kyle Ainsworth, Special Collections Librarian, East Texas Research Center, Stephen F. Austin State University, Nacogdoches, Texas for "Good Company" by Karle Wilson Baker, in *Blue Smoke: A Book of Verses* (New Haven: Yale University Press, 1919): p.19.

Margo Stipe, Curator and Registrar of Collections, Frank Lloyd Wright Foundation, Taliesin West, Scottsdale, Arizona, for Frank Lloyd Wright, *"The best friend of man on earth is the tree."*

****

Special Thanks to

My wonderful family for their encouragement and support

The authors who came before me with their beautiful sayings about trees

Stan Revis, the Real Forester, of the Tree Longevity Corporation

Jack Siebenthaler, Journalist, *Southern Nursery Digest*

Dr. Nicole Provost

The Gainesville office, Florida Department of Children and Families

Lisa Wroble, Institute of Children's Literature

My editors at MuseItUp Publishing:
Nancy Bell
Valerie Haley
Cover artist, Kaytalin Platt

Publisher of MuseItUp Publishing, Lea Schizas